The Last Witch
of Dogtown

A NOVEL BY

FRANCIS BLESSINGTON

Francis Blessington

THE CURIOUS TRAVELLER PRESS
GLOUCESTER, MASSACHUSETTS

THE CURIOUS TRAVELLER PRESS
a division of
The Pressroom Printers, Incorporated
32 Blackburn Center
Gloucester, Massachusetts 01930

Design and Digital production by

Kate Wollensak / k.a.wollensak design
Annisquam, Massachusetts

Printed in The United States of America

ISBN 1-892839-07-5

To Ann, Geoff, and Julia for walking these trails.

To Andrew —

Yang Writer

F. B   11.29.01

The infidels have hooted witchcraft out of the world.

— JOHN WESLEY

Dogtown is delusion.

— JOSEPH E. GARLAND

Also by
FRANCIS BLESSINGTON

POETRY

Lantskip

Wolf Howl

VERSE PLAY

Lorenzo de' Medici

VERSE TRANSLATIONS

Aristophanes: The Frogs

Euripides: The Bacchae

LITERARY CRITICISM

The Motive for Metaphor (ed. with Guy Rotella)

Paradise Lost and the Classical Epic

Paradise Lost: Ideal and Tragic Epic

The Last Witch of Dogtown

A NOVEL BY

FRANCIS BLESSINGTON

1829

CHAPTER 1

The village lay dying. Those early settlers might have known farms
would fail, when they first eyed this waterless headland covered with
immovable boulders, many bigger than our houses. Long ago the boulders crushed the woods and lured those headlong pioneers to pipe-
dream on the moors on Cape Ann. But even they couldn't foretell that
the Goose Cove Dam and Riverdale Bridge would be built and linked
by a road that would throw us into the byways. What prophet could
have imagined the rise of Gloucester, selling salted fish to Bonaparte's
army? More and more, those port people took our land to pasture their
cattle and wanted us off. Unlike most in the Commons Settlement, I
had a wife and boy, so I, "Granther" Halliday, descended from good
English yeoman family, had to drift from shoemaker to toothpuller to
coffin-maker to wagoner to worse.

I was carting mackerel from Gloucester back up the Fox Hill Road to our Commons Settlement, hoping the October sun was cool enough for the fish to keep and that folk were in pocket enough to sell to. The day was heating up, and I was dressed in black as always, like a preacher without a collar. I spouted sweat. The huge boulders were throwing heat like furnaces. Then to make matters worse, my oxen froze right in front of the cabin of Thomazine Younger, the witch. (Others called her Tam, but I wouldn't.) Trying to lash the team over Alewife Brook Bridge, I broke my switch.

No one was about. So I went to grab a fresh birch in the lot behind the wooden cabin. There I found a pile of bluing pumpkins sloping up like steps to her shuttered attic window. They looked like the smaller of our boulders now covered with fallen leaves. I didn't expect to sell much fish, and we were on the point of starving. Those pumpkins would only rot, and Thomazine had taken those squashes as tolls through her phony spells anyway. The old witch was nowhere about. My yellow St. John's retriever, Start, didn't bark or shy away from her house. He was a great noticer, like all those water dogs. If anyone were there, he'd know. From the bank of the brook, her geese shot at us, honking and hissing and ducking. But Start scattered them with a bark.

Glancing at the back window, I yanked a gourd from the bottom of the pile. Then a side stake gave way, and the pumpkins rumbled down from the house all the way down the slope into the brook, like the biblical swine. I ran for my team, but the window swung slowly open. I dropped the pumpkin, and it shattered at my feet. I sucked in air and stood still.

The superstitious said that Thomazine could kill a man with her spells and that for sure she had killed many cattle and prize sheep. No gun muzzle appeared: just the string that kept the window from opening too far.

I knew then what would happen. It happened to all the drivers who passed here. What made me think I was any different? Start raced off. I didn't dare call him. He didn't even bark. It was like a wet net fell over me and tightened. My skin bristled, and the soles of my feet tingled.

Like some burnt owl of hell, Thomazine appeared at the window and froze me with her green eyes. Although indoors on a hot day, she wore her black bonnet, while her dirty wisps of gray hair flew around her mug like salt hay. Her faded wool shawl was the color of sumac. She opened her great mouth, and her great upper teeth hung like icicles over a cave mouth. She pointed her witch finger at me: "Whoreson, I know you, Granther Halliday. I'm slow to git here now, but I'm a long way from dyin'. Yer behavin' like wharf scum. I was goin' to let yer pass nice, but then yer try to swipe my pumpkin. Go tend yer fuckin' beefies." She spat tobacco juice at me and banged the shutter.

I ran to the front of the house.

Before I reached my oxen, I could hear them bellowing. They were kneeling on the ground, their tongues licking dirt. My stomach jammed with cold, and I couldn't curse, my jaw was so stiff and shaky. My knees swayed, and I was about to faint. My legs stiffened with pain, all glass-like, and this has happened ever since.

Thomazine thundered out of the house and stalked toward the wagon. Her speed was always unnatural, even for a young woman. The eyes of the oxen were half shut, and they could not look up. She reached over the wagon side and flicked back the canvas tarp and delved deep and swung out between her two big mitts a half dozen mackerel from a dripping basket and swept back into the house without so much as looking at me.

My stiff legs began to stir, and I edged slowly toward the wagon, but stopped short, when again the door swung open. The old witch sailed out once more, her fat yawing from side to side. With her great, red hands, she hove up the yoke from under, and the oxen clambered up on their heavy feet in a maelstrom of gold dust. When she shot out her pointing finger, they rattled their harness, shambled across the bridge, and halted.

She broke off a hazel switch and held it out to me.

As I stepped forward to grasp it, she pointed it down toward the brook. I wanted to clout her, but my hands were tacked to my sides. I angled my glass legs down the slope and brought up the first pumpkin.

When I reached the top again, she shouted, "Carry two, lardass!" laughing like Old Nick.

I looked down. Many of the pumpkins were sunk in the brook water. I remembered--salt. It was said witches could be stopped with salt. With the last of my money, I had bought a box of sea salt at Gloucester for salting game. If I could reach the salt, maybe the superstition would quiet the witch. I grabbed the box and threw some salt on the ground beside the wagon. Thomazine came quick, tramping over the white grains, and took the salt box from me.

"Yer forgot to salt the fish, Granther." She disappeared into the house.

I skated down into the dark cleft of the mill brook and zagged back up with a pumpkin under each arm, slipping and catching myself everywhere on the steep gravel, dripping from the knees.

I shouted, "The devil take ye off, ye old faker!"

I saw no one but I heard from behind the shutter, "You'd make us a fine witch, Granther. Yer got the spunk."

I ignored her and waded back down into the stream.

Thomazine wandered out, sat on the wood pile, and cat-napped in the sun.

When I had finished stacking the squashes, I tried to reset the side stake. In spite of my years working with wood, I couldn't stable it. It was soft and bent rather than went down into the ground, or it fell, curved like a serpent onto the ground, like Aaron's rod. I was bedeviled all right. The worst of witchery was the shame of it: you were controlled by something else.

I no sooner had that thought than she awoke and stabbed me with her green eyes.

"How does the damned stake go?" I asked, giving in.

She knew her business and said nothing, just closed her eyes in the boiling sun. It was noon, and she cast no shadow.

Finally, I angled the stake in and went for my oxen.

As I passed Thomazine, I saw how much she had aged recently. Her face was deeply rutted from the wind and sun and salt. I decided to give her more of the fish. The village was as hard on her as it was on the rest of us, and, if she found a business, it was founded on Yankee ingenuity like others. What were half-rotting pumpkins going to do for her? She was dying, too, like the village.

But as I approached my team, I suddenly heard behind me the rumble again. I spun around but not quickly enough to see Thomazine get back. She was still preening in the heat, but she sure must have pulled out the stake, for the pumpkins were running back down into the brook.

Thomazine hissed obscenities that followed me down like the cursing of lunatics. I brought the pumpkins up again--like harridan heads. I restacked her squashes carefully, as if I were making a perfect stone wall, so I would not need the damn stake. If the village had made her peculiar it was not my lookout. Hours of steamy sun seemed to pass.

Finally she handed me the switch, and I got away.

As fast as I might, I lashed the team up the Fox Hill Road toward the Commons Settlement. Behind my wagon a screaming squall of gulls fluttered, dancing lightly on the tarp and pecking, till I waved my switch.

But they returned like the plague. Some zoomed over the oxen backs at my head-- the red spots on the bill flying by me like random drops of blood.

A horrible stench filled the air. I stopped and fought my way through the blizzard of gulls and pulled back the tarp. The fish had rotted and smelled like the old well where we threw the dead horses.

CHAPTER 2

Along a flyway of fish stench, I turned back to Gloucester. I was carting for Samuel Gilbert, a ship's outfitter on the corner of Front and Commercial, who also wholesaled fish. I could have dumped the fish into the harbor and lit out, but it grew on me that I had been duped into buying half-rotted fish. Well, I wasn't going to run. I'd go back and give him some mind.

When I went by Thomazine's, I blinkered the oxen so they didn't halt.

I stopped in front of Gilbert's shop. The wishbone bonnets who strolled past brought their handkerchiefs to their noses. Knowing the tune of his harness, Sam was already silhouetting the doorway, framed by tar buckets and block and tackle. He was a small, gray man.

"What are you doing, Granther? Get that stinking mess out of the road!"

"Thomazine stopped me," I began.

"Witchery! How can you blame witchery for this? Give her her bit like the other drivers and go on. I suspect you got drunk and left the tarp off the fish to cover up your drinking. Did you salt them?"

"You said they were fresh."

"But Granther, you can't take all darn day goin' about it. You kill the fish."

"They were dead when you gave them to me." I began to fling things like that at people often now, though long ago joking got me thrown out of Harvard College.

"Give up your job for a joke, Granther. That's you. Go rot in Dogtown! At least *I'll* not have to deal with you no more."

He reminded me of a squirrel that I once caught by the tail and that bit me. When you can't do something about something, you joke it. And his phony anger fired me up. I threw the reins in his face and jumped down from the wagon, holding my stick above my shoulders to strike him, but I thought of the Lord and relented.

Then the oxen rattled and started off.

To halt them, I shot out my witch finger accidentally and immediately they swung down on the road on their knees, almost breaking the shaft, licking dirt, just as at Thomazine's.

Pretending I was terrified, I jumped back as far as Sam did and the ladies with the handkerchiefs. He rushed back into his store, banged the till, came rushing back like a squirrel from his cache, and gave me twenty dollars, more than ten times what I owed for the fish, three cents each, and four bits a week for the wagon rental.

"Keep your damn witchery in the Commons."

The constable, a long drink of water named Call, was walking fast toward me. I walked toward the span of oxen and placed my hand under the yoke, as I had seen Thomazine do.

Without any effort of mine, they rose miraculously to their feet.

All looked on in amazement.

While the oxen blocked the constable's way, I ran off down the street.

I heard Sam yell, "Let trash go," as I ran, and being tired and forty-five did not slow me down till I was back on the Fox Hill Road again heading for the Commons Settlement, or Dogtown, as they were calling it now because of all the strays gathering there. As I repassed Thomazine's dirty hovel, I raised my switch in homage to her and thought of giving her some of the money but remembered the fish and pumpkins and thought we were more than even. She was nowhere in sight but was no doubt watching me from somewheres.

By then I was tiring. I turned down the road towards the Commons Square, which was nothing now but three paths crossing. Then I bent left down the Back Road. A flock of passenger pigeons broke off the sun. Across the bare landscape to the north, I could see greater boulders beyond those in the settlement: the billows of Ipswich Bay, like those we had seen for months in the crossing from Portsmouth. Now the few sheep, horses, cattle, and timber that we had and the mills were all gone and the headland drier than ever. We were never much more than wood lots and cow rights, anyhow. The land was ruled by barberries and fern. You can't farm dry land or herd well where stock get stuck between rocks or fall to their deaths. Between the Commons bars was the only safe pasture. For a while, we managed to prosper, till Boston burned up all our wood. Now only the feral dogs wandered our ghost town among the few remaining handkerchief patches of potato and corn.

The Indian-summer sun burned the scattered red-yellow maples that dotted the land. The shuttered windows on either side of the bible-leafed doors drew me back to the covered portholes and mother sick the whole voyage. I recalled the tired snowy owl that collapsed on the deck far at sea and how I and the other boys had tormented it with hoop sticks till it died and my mother threw the bloody duster over-board. I felt like that now. And these covered portholes, like our windows, couldn't keep out the snow. In winter, we swept the snow that drove in through the uncaulked cracks back out into the empty moorland. The monotony of the sea nearby and the monotone landscape oppressed me, as always.

My village was damned.

I fell asleep on one of the great rocks.

CHAPTER 3

It was dark when I awoke. In my half sleep, I heard several wagons pass. News of witchery travels faster and smells worse than the stench of fish. I braced myself for the worst at supper.

Though a good woman, Lizzy was of a ticklish disposition and was high taken with orthodoxy, her father (my uncle) having been a Presbyterian minister in Haverhill. Our marriage had been shaky. When I was expelled from Harvard College, she would have broken off our engagement, except I argued that just because I was unorthodox did not mean that she had any right to break a civil and religious contract. I also added that I feared what would happen to me. There was the family for her to face too. This gave her the excuse she needed to justify her love for me. But witchery terrified her. Since childhood,

Lizzy had dreaded Thomazine. Soon after our arrival in the Commons, Lizzy would visit us, and Thomazine would come and ask her to live with her. Later, her Haverhill cousins would torment her by telling her that Thomazine Younger was coming to take her away. The poverty of our village had made her worse, and now she was pregnant again to boot. So she was always clamoring to go to the Harbor Village of Gloucester. And she was right. What future did we have in the village? But a diferent destiny awaited us.

I had to brace myself too for dealing with my morose son—now sixteen, fat, and friendless, always thorny and now getting worse, strutting idly about in fine black Spanish-leather boots, which I made. There were few youths to sport with now, few odd jobs to do, since I and the few others needed them. Till recently, like other boys, Scot would ride the cattle in the Commons. The oxen especially did not mind. Since water was scarce, the sun had often yellowed the grass to inedibility before the cattle could finish it of a summer. The youngsters would loll, bored, in the dead grass, while the cattle looked for shade that was hard to find. The children stared up at the clouds and told what kinds of boats they resembled: fishing schooners, seiners, pinkies, dories, brigs, barkentines. Boats of all sizes sailed in the blue sky that was often free of the summer dust that hovered over most towns around, for the winds that gathered around the headland were constant. The boys gigged and skinned frogs in the lowlands and brought them up to grill on a small fire made for the purpose, or they set fires in the woods, which would have to be quickly quelled with the cistern water we saved, or our cabins were in danger. I saw how Lizzy had withered with poverty from the woman who danced solo to the viola at huskings, her arm and shoulder movement the most expressive of all her sex, and who made love to me beside our blueberry pails on Raccoon Ledge. With the decline of the village, all this world died away.

While I was eating cabbage and gravy soup in the diurnal smoldering silence, Scot blurted, "I hope you aren't going to the witches,

Father." My rebellion against smirking orthodoxy—our yeoman family trait for centuries—rekindled. But how could I tell them that I loved and wanted to save them. And who was I to save anyone?

So I said, "Dogtown was always delusion. Even Reverend Davis gets lost among the woods and huge boulders."

Scot jerked his head up and shot a look at Lizzy, "That's 'cause we're bewitched, like those oxen."

Lizzy slammed her feet. "Stop! Stop talking in that ungodly way," she shouted. Then she changed her tune: "Yes, father will ruin us all, and you'll never get a place in the Harbor."

But Scot turned on her, "Leave Father alone." The sudden reversal stunned and consoled me. I wanted to reach out to him—and her.

Instead, I added, "Witchcraft is nonsense."

Trembling, Lizzy snapped at me: "Maybe so. Then them that does it is mighty ridiculous. I heard about the oxen in the Harbor Village. Are you going mad?"

I cried, "For God's sake, Lizzy!" I heard my voice, as if it were someone else's. Possession. Maybe this is possession: this thwarting of one's nature—that was the real invasion of the Devil, wanting to do what you couldn't.

Desperate, she rattled on, "The madness of witchcraft. Stop it, please, stop! It's so darn tedious!"

But I couldn't. A spasm of anger hurled me against them like a poltergeist. Afraid of its power, I shoved the plate of cabbage away, banged the door, and stalked to my Boo, that is, my booth, my workshop, my temple to myself.

Another ax would fall, I knew it. You cannot be non-conformist long in New England without repercussions. Even in this tract of rocky desolation, the long arm of orthodoxy reaches for your throat. Someone walked about outside the Boo. I looked stealthily out the window. It was Scot making sure I was all right.

That month our fifth child, Cora, was born dead, like the three before Scot. The midwife showed it to me: a head of curly black hair on a broken doll I could not mend. I had not seen the other deaths. We were lucky, I told Lizzy, trying in vain to console her: one child living was more than most hoped. Rev. Henry and Belle had lost four and had no other. But Lizzy was bowed-down lower than ever, while I held in. Scot preoccupied her, so I kept even more time at the Boo. There was nothing that could be said. We had to get out.

CHAPTER 4

But we had neither prospects nor money for leaving the village, and neither family nor bank would lend. The Gloucester Bank would buy us out for under a hundred dollars now, if that, for our cabin values were dropping. So we couldn't go anywhere else, except be a burden to the Haverhill relations. We hung on.

When the sleety January ocean wind was blowing down necks, Thomazine asked me to come and bring my dentist gear. When I arrived at her cabin, I expected to see the hag I had seen a few months ago. But she had healed herself of the ravages of age. Her recently gray face now shone like a polished doubloon. Looking ten years younger, she sat on a stool at her puncheon table, finishing one of my mackerel, now salted. She was savoring my anger more than my fish.

I snapped at her: "Thomazine, toothache doesn't pain your appetite none."

"Granther," she grunted, "These fishes have lovely tiny teeth, not like these"—she unlipped her mouth and pointed to her giant blackening canines with her fork—"and they pain me now, as they grit down."

"They look awful, but the roots retract, you know."

She was putting herself in my power. If she were a witch, why did she need my science? She had made herself look younger. She went on eating the bones and head and all. She nodded for me to sit beside her on the stool. We sat on two of the three stools that Thomazine owned.

"I'm no beaver or werewoman or even a witch. I scare people for no reason with these teeth, like some bulldog who wants to be friendly. That's why they call me witch."

She looked at me with sheepish, reddened eyes. I thought of the oxen gasping but remembered my own spell and thought I might be a match for her. But there was real pain in that leathery face too, young as it now looked.

She must have been half-intoxicated, for she rambled now. She began to talk of her niece who lived with her: "Judy Rhines 's run off to live with that escaped Louisiana slave Black Neil, who must have more voodoo than either Judy or me. I'm left alone now. I need her back."

"You want a toothpuller or a witch?"

"The teeth are paining me. I can't think right, when such like that happens."

"But if you're a witch."

Clear-minded now, she clawed my arm. I felt in her the strong muscle of her power. "The first lesson in witchery is you learn what you can't do."

I looked into her endless green eyes and said nothing.

I had never been inside her lair. I glanced about the room. She watched me look and smiled content and passed into a trance. A large wooden pestle and a large marble mortar—for grinding potions? A mattock, though Thomazine did no outside work. Did she dig holes in the graveyard to get shrouds and corpses? The large book with wooden covers and silver clasps, was it a Bible or the Black Book or her own Book of Shadows? In the fire bucket was conspicuously placed a grub hoe with black ribbons. It would serve for a witch's wand. On a sideboard were dried herbs I couldn't identify.

Thomazine awoke and quickly got up. Again her speed was supernatural for an old she-devil. She brought to the table corn bread, butter, and cider. I rose to help, but she patted me down. "Have to do it all my damned self, now. No fucking help left," she sighed.

While I ate, she took out her pipe and lit her tinder with one tap of the flint. She lit the pipe with a long match and let the smoke wreathe her head like a bonnet. The smoke had an acrid smell. Then she began coughing and sat on a greasy, stained yellow settee, where she managed to get her breath. She lolled her head back.

The acid in the smoke took hold of her. She began to weave her head around and babble and cry: "I ain't no werewoman or fucking beaver. 'Sides Judy's the real witch. I don't want none of these bastards around hereabouts making out like I'm the sort Judy Rhines is—a whore. You know she is, Granther. Don't look that way. Judy Rhino: her choppers are bigger than mine. Or that Black Neil, the Black Man hisself he is, bewitchin' Jude to run off and live with him and them no longer young either."

I put a piece of cornbread in my pocket and rose to go. "Gab about your teeth another day, Thomazine."

But she snapped her head off the settee and spoke clear as a bell: "Jude's a witch for true, full of mockery and damnation." she said. "Saw these aching dogs off, Granther, please!"

She opened her mouth. I moved close and looked in. Even worn flat, they looked like the great rocks of Whale's Jaw. Her breath smelled worse than the rotted mackerel.

"You know that crazy coot Neil shaves with an ax?"

Still on Black Neil. I smelled the rat. Why not flush it out and put her on the run? Judy left figuring she had a chance with Black Neil, instead of listening to that damn moaning, like the monotonous sea around Cape Ann. I can't stand moanin'. Maybe your village is dying out, but moanin' don't do no good.

"She's your niece, almost a daughter."

"No matter. True witch, let me tell you, but too full of damned mockery. But the teeth: hack 'em off," she said, still chewing and opening her mouth and pointing. They were grand.

"Ain't oak saplings, Thomazine. I'd slice the nerve clean through and you'd die of shock."

"Then yank 'em out."

I needed the money, if she ever would pay me. "Sure. Any dire in the house?"

Thomazine never blinked like another woman would and pretend not to know the local potion that Aunt Rachel Smith made. She had a flask near. I knew that. Thomazine just went straight into the larder and got a jar. After a dram, she propped up some greasy bolsters on her faded settee and lay back, ready for the operation.

"Sure you want it this way, Thomazine? If you were a seal, you would die without your ice-cutters."

She slowly closed her eyes and mumbled, "A seal! Granther, your whore-faced jokes have made you poor." She leaned back and, dazed from the smoky drug and dire, soon dozed again.

Sure, my joking ways cost me a good bit, like the carting job or my impersonating a visiting bishop from Scotland once, while I was at Harvard College. I always looked beyond my years—called "Grandfather," "Granther," even in school—so I performed an imposture by dressing like an Episcopal bishop no one had seen, but who was known to wear a beard, thick glasses, and to lisp. Made up as for the stage, I was fed and wined in the High Church manner for two days, even though I had to mumble when I messed up part of the litany of churching a woman after childbirth. Still, my ruse went undiscovered.

It wasn't until a delegation arrived from Saint Andrews that the sham came out—some jealous student must have peached. I would have been sent down then, but the whole business was so embarrassing, my teachers hushed it up. No doubt that joke led to my dismissal the following year. But Thomazine had no right to remind me of such things. She needed me to take out her dogs and get Judy back. Well, she'd pay.

"Two dollars, Thomazine." I looked straight into her green beads.

That woke her. "That's twice the pinch of a pound of tea." She gripped the sides of the foul settee.

"Take it, or keep your chisels." I turned to leave.

"Give you a dollar come Easter." Her eyes swam, and she winced.

I said, "Then we wait."

"One-fifty."

"Two firm. And no spells on carts for a year. Else—goodbye now."

Thomazine smirked: "Amen." She shut her eyes with sudden indifference.

She fumbled in her many skirts, and got two dollars out of somewhere and put them on the settee beside her.

Her mystery lured me on.

Out of my satchel, I took my pincers, a new pair just picked up at the new Topsfield Fair at the tooth-pulling show. Quite a few gulls had shown up that year to watch, and it outdrew the sheep-dog trials, so the barber needed a helper to pull teeth and entertain the penny oglers. I had "forgotten" to return the pincers, just as he "forgot" to pay me. A good pair they were too, for I heard the barber dislocated several jaws using the other pair he had to use after I left.

I grabbed a towel from the rack beside the sink, wrapped it around her neck, and tilted her head back.

I saw Thomazine's hand slide out and slip the money back where shame would keep me from going after it.

So I drew down one eyetooth about half-way. Then I drew the other down to match it. Thomazine didn't even notice. She was half drunk now and braced for the release and the pouring down of the blood. Well, she did look like a werewoman, making Judy Rhines' teeth look small as a hen's. My hilarity gave way to something else—some getting at the root of things, not just teeth. A sense of fishing in troubled waters.

I left the teeth half out. "Best I can do, Thomazine," I said, putting away the pincers and clicking my black bag shut.

Half-delirious, thinking her teeth were out, she drove her long fangs into her lower lip. "Damfthnation! Youf ukin dumaff." She went on in profusion. She was in a tantrum, jumping around spitting blood all over the settee and the bolsters and her dirty sumac shawl. Real tears rutted her face.

"Peace, peace," I shouted. "I'll pull them, but, remember, no more spells on wagons for a year. And don't forget the two dollars." Now, if Thomazine had been a complete witch, rather than the swamp mouth that she was, she would have made me into a woolly bear caterpillar and crushed me or yanked her own teeth out, for she never relented or bargained, but she was losing blood and mind fast.

She threw her witch pointer at me, trying to mumble magic or foul words, but the fangs just dug into her jaw. I was overcoming the Queen of the Witches.

"Stop, Thomazine!"

Finally she reached into her wools and came out with the dollar bills.

She was a strong woman, but with one hand I pressed her forehead back on the settee and sat on her chest. I tugged down and out one dog tooth. Then the other as fast as I could. I stuffed the largest cotton wad I had into her mouth. As I pocketed the money, she swung her cuss finger at me. My legs stiffened to glass again.

The glass in my legs set me off further on the chase. I was struggling with Thomazine's witchery, tugging it, holding it, loving it. What powers did it have? What I could do with such power, such fakery. Yet my legs were glassy from her powers. If I had some such power, I sure wouldn't be a petty thief, like Thomazine. Maybe I could blackmail her with Judy's return into coming to Meeting, where Thomazine hadn't been for years. But now she was now spluttering on about damnation so, she probably would have welcomed the idea of Hell. Certainly if Thomazine could not bear Judy's taking up with Black Neil, I could work around that somehow. Or Thomazine had lost her power over her, or Judy was the greater witch. Maybe I could finally do some good in this fallen world, but not as a minister of God. I was full of myself. But Thomazine's bleeding, foul mouth was proof that witches, if they had any powers, were not all-powerful, as she said. Wrestling these teeth was intoxicating, my own powers doubled as if they emanated from her housecoats foul with earth and sweat and extorted money. I was breathless with the thrill of her now, the smell and power of her blood.

When all was over, Thomazine had no mind to cast one of her phony spells. I had won her. She struggled up off the settee, holding her towel to her bleeding mouth.

"Keep your chin up, Thomazine," I said, softly now, wiping the blood from her chin with the towel. "Keep your big, bony chin up."

I had triumphed.

She said no more, being too fainty.

When I stepped outside, the January sleet slammed against me.

By instinct, I reached into my pocket. The bills were gone! She had picked my pocket, even in her delirium.

I went back toward the door, but her geese charged me again, blocking the door, squawking, hissing, necks lowered, jaws open with hate. I slung one over my back, like Saint Nick, figuring she had owed me more than that, considering stealing the mackerel and making me lose that job and gain a reputation for witchery to boot.

But I had forgotten the witch's great speed. I was just out of sight of her cabin on the first bend of the Fox Hill Road, when Thomazine herself flew out of the wet brush and sleet, waving the ribboned grub hoe, blood still bubbling from her mouth. In spite of my glassy legs, I hoofed away from her, and soon she was out of sight.

As I turned into the Settlement, however, Thomazine again leapt into the road, this time on all fours and barking like the tide, her chin clean as a boulder.

Her coming at me so sudden and her dog act, so frighteningly real, made me lose heart. I smashed the goose in her face, and she fell over backwards muttering her wicked prayers.

I heard her groan, "Tell Judy to came back."

Her suffering overcame me, and her fiendish energy. She believed in me in her zany's way. What had she seen in me? Was she really passing the mantle? I had found her wounded and could make it hurt more or try to cure her.

I stopped. I cried out, "Should Judy Rhines come back with Neil?"

Still on all fours, she stared blankly a moment. "Yes, yes, with Neil," she barked and pawed me. Then called, "Granther."

"What?"

"Belle thinks the world of you. She does." Then she burst into laughter.

Isabel Davis was the beautiful wife of the minister. She was baiting me with hell and witchery.

I felt in my pocket and found the bills were there again.

The times were making us delirious.

CHAPTER 5

The next day the sleet had stopped, and the day was bright with brittle cold.

I looked at the bills and found they were drawn on a Georgia bank. I hardly dared go to the Harbor Village, but debts were high and we hadn't a crust. I had long used up the twenty dollars from Sam Gilbert. Since no one wanted shoes repaired or teeth pulled or coffins made, I put off my robe of shame and walked to the Gloucester Bank, the same bank that would lend us nothing but would buy us out for a song.

The Gloucester Bank was a fort, quarried from wrecked farm-houses, leveled and molded into Respectability. Respectability was keeping us in Dogtown and ruining the country everywhere, and the keystone to Respectability is a bank.

When I arrived, I slipped past Constable Call, who was on guard, asleep on his feet in the frosty sun. I didn't need him to recognize me from the farce with the oxen.

I went in. In the rear of the great room, the silver-haired president of the bank, Epes Wilson, sat signing what were probably bank mortgages. He turned around and looked at me, to see if I came to sell my plot. Not yet, Shylock.

Years ago, abandoning his old house, my friend Abram Wharf went rabid with cabin fever, drink, and righteous zeal at the tactics used by the Harbor to refuse us work and squeeze us into selling our land. Abram burst into the bank with a dueling pistol and shouted at the old pirate who was then president, "This is the end of your usury, Old Shylock." What did they expect from us anyway? The old president jumped up and yelled, "Not by a damn sight," and leveled him with his fists; then he called, "Hurry, the directors are on their way. Haul the damn corpse out," though Abram was still alive. After that, bank presidents kept Abram's loaded pistol on the desk, as a paperweight. That's Respectability in a nutshell. If you need something to hate, a bank president does just fine. The bank always had it in store for us.

The great room was all polished walnut and brass, like a new tavern. The clerks were all young. They wouldn't have hired me anyway, since I was "Dogtown" now, beyond the pale of Respectability.

I swallowed hard and walked up to a fat teller who had put on a fresh collar that morning. I remembered fishing with him at Fresh Pond a few times. Once when our lines got tangled, he stole some fish off my line.

"I found these bills in one of the cellars up in the Commons— Dogtown—are they any good?"

The teller asked, "Was there an ox standing on them?"

I swallowed hard.

I heard a laugh behind him.

He spoke for the benefit of his red-headed friend, the second clerk, smaller and thinner, who was stacking coins and who just washed his red hair with soap so that it had facets like slate.

The fat boy, whose name was Roger, chuckled at his own jest.

I gripped the bars to tear the cage out of the wood, but he had taken the money and had passed it on to the president who sat facing the wall, Abram's pistol beside him and showing only his stone-colored hair. He didn't turn one of those hairs, just caressed the pistol butt, balancing accounts, taking over.

The redhead stacking coins asked me, "Many long nights up in Dogtown lately?"

My creek was full and running over. I fired back, "Do you know why you're better than the blessing of God?"

The clerk squinted up at me, contemptuous-like.

"Well, son, you know, really nothing is better than the blessing of God. Isn't that right."

"Yes, sir," he said, staring at the coins in front of him on the table.

"Well, you're better than nothing, aren't you?"

Red waited for more.

Then from the president's desk, the fat clerk guffawed more at me than with me, and the soaped hair bobbed and glared at me. The pirate slammed the pistol on the desk.

The red-haired clerk whispered, "Shut up, Roger."

The pistol slammed again.

I shot my witch finger out again, the redheaded boy swung his hands up before his face to make the cross, and his hands struck the coins and sent them flying.

The president still didn't turn a hair, just curled his finger on the trigger. Roger still stood at attention beside the president's desk.

The old pirate picked up the pistol and cocked it. He whispered, still looking at the wall: "Your name?"

Recalling my friend's incident, I shouted, "Abram Wharf!"

The old pirate whirled and aimed the pistol at me.

I could hear only my own breathing, but I kept looking right into the pistol barrel.

The constable came from behind and bent my arm double. The few customers flurried out, and the clerks flung themselves up against the walls.

The president looked cool again and snorted: "Dare you defraud a bank?"

"Not at all," I said. "My name is Morgan Halliday. I meant to say: 'Abram Wharf needs the money,' for he helped me raise my Boo and I haven't given him his two dollars."

The old pirate put the pistol down and asked, "Your Boo?"

Red added under his breath, "Witch's den."

The constable twisted the answer out of my arm: "Workshop up in the Commons."

"Devil's workshop," Red added.

The steel head nodded.

"Money's good," Roger said, handing me two new bills.

Humiliation drove me on. I turned to Red, who was still picking up coins on the floor: "Can you change these? Abram won't have use for such large bills."

Fat Roger laughed but seemed a little worried. I figured their positions were new and still shaky in the bank, so they couldn't throw too much hay around.

Roger snatched the bills and handed them down to Red who handed him up the new coins from the floor.

"Don't forget the new commission," the pirate said. "Two bits."

My anger burned blue.

Red handed me the reduced money, which I ashamedly took.

"I think you should go now and pay Mr. Wharf," the president said.

Getting in between me and the teller cage, the constable began to nudge me out, as I looked at the money in my hand.

The constable gave me a shove out the door, or I would have bitten the president, pistol or no pistol.

As I quit the bank, I could hear the constable stalking me, closing in behind, sense the heat of his breath even in the cold. Damned if I would even now give him the satisfaction.

A slash of pain tore my left ear and neck.

I fainted.

Seconds later, I came to. My coins were in the street. My head washed with surf. The street was empty but for the constable.

He shouted, his long jaw shaking: "That's the cure for witchery! More of that and there'd have been less of it all along. Behave next time you come to a nice town like this. Why can't you act like other people—and at your age? Go back and live with your dogs! And keep your damned spells outa here."

CHAPTER 6

Skull whirring, I gathered my coins and stumbled on my glass legs toward the Commons Settlement. The pain. Stumbled off on the wrong trail. It was snowing. Yes, paths deluding. Light dust of snow blinds and ships you off to Sandy Bay, when you want the Commons.

Three thousand acres makes up just Dogtown, doesn't it? Let alone the rest of the headland. Hermits, outlaws live years unseen among rocks and twiggy trees. Where were my markers? Ears belling.

In spite of the cold I lost consciousness, sitting against a rock. The pain in my neck and a dog yowl roused me before I froze.

It was dark and probably late. When I stood up and stepped out in front of the boulder, the cold, sodden Atlantic wind tore at me, but the snow had stopped.

Cattle or rocks seemed to stir.

I saw a light in a ruined cellar hole beneath the old Lurvey house. Probably that crazy coot Black Neil believing still that there was treasure under the old ruin and digging in the cold with his ax.

I walked the road to the Commons Square where carts had packed down the snow. On my right, in the Town pasture, the dogs were gathering, dogs orphaned by the deaths of widows. The relentless baying drowned even the voices from the surrounding sea, the voices it was said of all who had drowned there around Cape Ann. Black Neil said that witches call the dogs into the Commons at night to harass the cattle and so tire the dogs that the witches can tame them for their own purposes. He said the dogs were the village's army against the ravages of the town.

Sure enough, amidst the dogs and dark and snow, I spotted Thomazine Younger, romping full of dire in the cold moonglow, as indifferent to the cold as Neil, swinging her flabby arms, like a zany.

When the wind died down. I could hear her, though she pretended not to see me.

"Beloved," Thomazine said to an Eskimo dog, "is it you? You who were faithful when my husband wouldn't open the door to me, chased by the town? The night you first had me in bed without my husband. Small as you are, you held the lash and drove me to your pen, the only faithful voice in the county."

She answered herself in a man's voice, as if she were in a one-person play: "Yes, I, King of the Dead, was there. I brought back your dead child to see you and would have brought your husband—if you had wanted him still."

Thomazine's answered, "Your voice is moving from dog to dog to dog. Why, if you love me, cannot I have you tonight?"

Her man voice said. "Someone's coming. I hear his step in the road."

Thomazine asked, "Another seaman's widow wanting her drowned husband and ready to sign the pact?"

"Think not," her male incubus voice growled. "What do you want?" it asked me.

Command performance, Thomazine making up all this mad pother—she who never had husband or child.

I decided to play the game. It might relieve my pain and gloom somehow. I wanted to become someone else, to escape. I pretended I was Black Neil. "I am no seeker of Samuel's shade. I want the gold, the gold."

"Whose gold?" Thomazine asked.

"Dogtown gold," I knew the new name would insult her, the dogs all milling about us now and muzzling up at her. "What's hidden in the cellars hereabouts. What cellar's it in?"

"Why you want it?" Thomazine asked, her incubus voice shaking.

I said, "I needs quit-rent. My soul wants to be free of hog slaying, cattle skinning, boat clerking. I'm one damned slave."

Thomazine's voice shook: "Why don't you keep on working?"

"Gold is here for the digging! Captain Kidd's gold." I said. "Where's it at?"

"In the cellar hole, the cellar hole."

I loved her grip on people. All danced her tune. There must be something in it.

A pine torch flared. I stiffened.

Maybe Thomazine's really got an incubus. But it wasn't a man. It was a long black shoulder cape, fluttering below the waist, and a black bonnet with a long pointed nose that reached to the bonnet's edge.

Lizzy.

She swept closer and held her torch to my eyes, almost singeing my hair. I could see the white terror in the face and the trembling of her narrow lips, as if she would cry. Thomazine blurred away into the dark and blowing snow, and the dogs howled and leapt about us.

Lizzy swallowed her tears and snarled, "Where have you been till this hour? What you doin' here in the dark cold with her? Witchery has made you all lunatic!"

She turned and sped home.

The snow began again in larger white flakes. Instinct alone led me slowly through the thick snow. My ear belled again, and I went the wrong way. By the time I got home, the cabin was empty and dark and the fire banked. I sent up the fire.

Lizzy had taken her carpet bag and Scot and left.

All that night, I cried my self helpless with prayer. At dawn I reminded myself that I still had powers.

I vowed I would bring her back.

CHAPTER 7

The snow pounded all night and was two feet deep by the purple dawn.

Even sitting by the fire, I shivered. How on such a night could Lizzy and Scot manage the three miles to Gloucester? She must have been mad herself. Everyone was now doing desperate things.

Someone banged on my door. I could barely push it open against the driving wind and piled snow.

Inside a huge green, wool cloak was Judy Rhines. I could only see the hair, like untamable wires, that barred her face.

"Granther, is Neil here?" She looked about. "He didn't come back last night. He'll die of cold."

I couldn't let her find to my shame that Lizzy and Scot had left.

But God had sent me something to take my mind away from them.

"Come in. Come in, Jude. Lizzy and Scot are visiting Goody in Haverhill."

She threw back her hood. Her cheeks were white with early frost bite. I sat her in front of the fire and made her tea with rum.

It did not take long to figure it. It was Thomazine who had sent Black Neil looking for the Dogtown gold again last night to get him away from Judy Rhines and then tried to get her to come back. She probably tried to heave a spell on him.

"Did Thomazine visit you last night?" I asked.

"Yes, she came after Neil went out. She wanted me to come back and live with her again. I threw a glamour on her, and she couldn't remember why she had come."

"You stay here by the fire and let the sting out. I'll find Neil. He's at the—" I knew then he was probably buried in the snow. Maybe dead. "I'll find him."

As I threw on my blue army frock coat, Judy pulled from her waistband a small leather bag with a drawstring and pressed it into my hand.

"Black henbane. Don't be afraid to use it." She shoved my hand into my pocket. "Call on Almodel," she added. "Please, please, hurry."

"Do you have something for your face? It's half frost."

"I'm coming, too."

"No Jude," I pleaded to no avail. "O.K. You check Philemon's Tavern. He may have passed out on the road there."

She nodded and ran off.

The cold snap came on fast. The New England sun was bandaged by the clouds, and the air was stiff and dark, one of those winter days when purple and gray are the only colors and cats freeze to death. Flakes the size of rags fell upon the huge boulders. I prayed that Lizzy and Scot had made it to Haverhill all right and that Neil was still alive in the Lurvey Cellar.

Through the thin woods, I soon saw the leaning wreck of the

Lurvey House through the thick lines of falling snow.

Below the two remaining joists was a mound of snow. I brushed it away. There Black Neil lay dead still and mud-encrusted in the open cellar hole. He lay in the lee of the cellar hole, half protected by the few remaining floor boards. His face was ashen above his worm-eaten blanket, his moleskin vest, and bare arms.

"You'll die here sleepin' in the goddam' cold!" I shouted down.

Nothing.

I lowered myself in the slippery snow.

I shouted again: "You'll freeze to death, witch!"

Neil still didn't answer, and my aching legs shot with cold and made me scream louder: "They'll cut your feet off!"

Before my stiff legs could reach him, Neil swung an arm across his eyes to block the dull light. The whole foolish business about finding buried treasure was going to kill the bastard.

Eyes blood-red, he stared blearily up.

His ax lay beside him and the holes chopped in the ground, indented in the snow, and the empty bucket of dire. "There ain't no Captain Kidd's treasure buried here, old fool."

Neil's eyes flickered and went out. His lips parted, his great horse teeth flashed in pain, and his big face shuddered.

The snow scrunched above us.

The minister's wife, Belle Davis, came slipping into the cellar hole, coughing in the cold, her red-gold, graying hair haloing her face outside her black wishbone bonnet, her green cape flowing over her maroon cloak, calling "Granther, what?"

"Neil's frozen," I whispered.

"God, no! Are we all going to die here?"

We knelt over Black Neil whose lips bowed stiffly into a mocking smile.

"Your feet, Neil. Please, for God's sake, be careful. The bitter cold!" Belle said.

She bent down, batted off the snow, and slipped off his torn shoes. I looked hard at the broken counters. I couldn't fix them this time. The welt edge was salt-rotted, and the soles half-ripped off. Like the Magdalen, Belle hugged his bare feet, though it made her quake with chill.

I began to rub Neil's half-frozen bare arms. I opened my coat and lay across him.

I saw fresh yellow vomit beside Neil.

He fainted again.

Must cure him—he'll die! I broke the black henbane leaves in my pocket, squeezed out some oil, smeared it on Neil's cheeks, stuffed some up his nostrils, crazily murmuring "Almodel, Almodel." What else could be done? I stared at Neil's scars, old dog bites streaked one cheek white, like tadpoles. "Dogs'll kill him," I said.

Belle looked away. Her husband, the Reverend Henry Davis was leading the campaign against the superstitions of witchery, blaming that for our ills. She often looked away like that when he preached.

Neil smiled a cracked lip. The henbane was working: his face unlaced.

Black Neil sat up: "Warm winter, B-B-B-Belle. F-F-F-F-Feet fresher than a salted c-cod," he said and coughed a gob of yellow spit.

But he was reviving.

"Too damp and stormy, Neil. God, those dog bites too!" Belle said, raising her head, her long lashes lit with snow, above her doe-like eyes, where great brown bears wandered on arctic ice floes. Belle and Henry Davis were among the few that stayed in the Commons now. They had fled England because of some scandal. Used to the high life of the golden town houses of Bath, Belle must have felt deserted among the huge rocks and tiny cottages of the village.

"You'll wake up dead," she said to Neil, "snowing bad now."

Neil grinned wider. I felt my own feet dancing.

"What dreams I have, Granther," he said, rapidly spitting two yellow gobbets. "I sometimes see those dogs tearing one lost nigger slave, 'scaped from Loosiana."

"Them's rabbit dreams," I snarled. "You're chasin' witch dollars, you are."

The three of us felt warm now.

"There's treasure in the Commons, Granther. Gonna find it, too. But you see no sky in the po'house. Why, they make me wear shirts there, sir warlock."

I relented. "True. That's why I work, old Neil, 'cause they make you a mess of their own in that place."

Neil tried to laugh, but his stiff face barely wrinkled. "I'm too old to go on with witchery like you. Where you get that stuff? Jude?"

"If Jude's around, you're not dying today. Let's get us out of this shitty hole," I said.

Neil said, "Like coming outa a grave, ain't it?"

I unstooped with pain into the purple light, but the sight of Neil living and strong gave me strength. My magic had taken hold.

CHAPTER 8

One night later, sharpening my awls at the Boo, I heard a strong rapping on the door.

The ever-ripe Moll Jacobs.

She once plied her trade with Judy Rhines; now she went about mostly alone, since Judy stayed in the village with Black Neil. She wore a blue wool shoulder cape edged in gold thread that touched the ground. With two fingers, she held up a pair of gold pumps, the only pumps in the village. They were down at heel.

While I reheeled the shoes, she sat slumped in my German peasant chair. This was my vanity: a black walnut stool from Germany with no arms and a tall, thin back with the inlaid carving of a stag raised in flight, looking back over his shoulder at you. I liked it better than the bar-backed ebony chairs, for their shape reminded me of the old heating chairs for witches. The peasant chair seemed to mock the sitter and was so uncomfortable no one stayed in it too long.

She lit a cigar and blew the smoke up the small spire of darkness above us. The startled stag carved on the back of the peasant chair must have been more erect than usual. Moll said nothing, just showed her black silk leg.

I set to work at once. She watched me minutely.

Finally she said: "May I smoke?" though she was already steaming like a sugar house.

"Yes, sir, keeps the bugs out."

She laughed a little too hard: "Bugs in this cold!" Her smoke came back down, hovering about in the still air, making it look like we were under water. It had a sweet licorice smell.

"Any news from Lizzy?" There were no secrets in the village. She opened her cape more and showed a low, green silk dress. The heat in the tiny, iron stove was almost out, and I was shaking.

"She writes that she's returning soon," I lied, hoping for some word.

"Why did she go?"

"Feeling poorly. She went to have Mother Goody take care of her."

"Isn't it odd that she would go off with Scot in this cursed weather if she felt dumpy?" She moved her face within inches of mine and reeked of perfumed powder. She blew pretend smoke in my face and laughed.

"Well, I don't know." I ripped off the old heels with the claw hammer so violently I almost tore her nose off. But she didn't flinch. She was a rough one.

She pushed me: "I mean if someone's ill, they usually think last of traveling." She blew a pillow of smoke above my head.

It was out anyway, so I said, "I think she's stung by my witchcraft doin's in the Harbor." I put down her pumps and stared at her, my empty hands dangling helpless.

"Judy told me you were trying your wings. You'll fly alone now. That's all. Like the rest of us."

"It got me nowhere, " I said, nonchalantly, but seeing Neil rise from the snow.

I picked up one pump and started to measure new heels with my eye.

I said, "Witchcraft *does* sometimes help, doesn't it?"

"Oh, I renounced helping long ago," she said laughing. Then added, "I guess I help in my way, though." She laughed again, harder.

I asked, "What do *you* believe in?"

"I believe in love, Granther." She rubbed my leg.

"Yes, I needed an amulet. It's working."

She laughed again. "No joking. It's not what you're thinking. I mean some kind of healing that we all need, that I can give. It makes us one, Granther, need does. It makes us all one—coven!"

I looked up into her great face, so close above mine. Red-gold ringlets were wet across her forehead. I bent down again. I could hear, and see, and smell her deep licorice breath. I caught her hand and moved it slowly away from my thigh, but I still stared into the canyon of her low flounced green dress.

"This is free," I said.

She moved away slowly, keeping her eyes on me, watching for some sign of weakness or need.

But I went back to her pumps, listening to my rasp and keeping my eyes bolted to the work. I could hear she was sliding around in her seat. When I was just setting the taps, I could feel her get out of her chair and stand over me, the startled stag staring at her grand buttocks. When I looked up, she held out her bare breasts and held them cupped for me, like soft pyramids of power. She pressed a hardened nipple into my parting lips.

"Mother's magic," she said, smiling into my soul.

Yes. That it was it, the flow of energy from thing to thing, from person to thing, from ocean to rock, as from Thomazine's hand clawing my arm. I needed that—but not from her, not now, not that way. It had to originate from me. I could have made love to her or left her to herself. I looked up at her: her eyes were shut, her pink, wet mouth partly opened, as if she were singing in a chorus of devils. But I could hear nothing but her breath whispering and offering her best—and that was not enough. She fingered each nipple, and I felt her heat over the cold in the Boo. A ripple of chill flowed down my back and down my legs, which lost their glass, and my member shot with blood. Yet I was the peasant-chair stagman himself, gaining a fort of advantage. I felt no longer powerless. There was a click of control, as if over a mule. Then cold shivered too strongly through my blood. I could barely sit because of the shaking. What if it were Belle...?

"Lizzy said she may be back tonight," I gasped.

Moll pulled back, pouted, rebuttoned. I handed her the retapped shoes. She smiled a tired, old-world smile.

But she had shown her magic, which was all magic, and was but overreaching another. Lying with her would have been mere gratitude now.

"Sure, Granther. If she doesn`t come, remember me, old Moll," she said, adding with a smile of condescension, "Off to the Harbor, where I *can* help."

She raised me and kissed me warm with her long tongue. I was passive.

I had won. Where it would lead was the excitement. My mind was full of expectation, though dizzy from the heavy smoke that still hung in the Boo. I watched her leave like a hungry kitten, but said nothing. Façade was all.

"Off to the Harbor" rang in my ear after she had gone. Had Lizzy said that in her way? What if Lizzy had now run off with Abram Wharf who asked her once? At first the thought knotted my stomach with cold. Then I felt a great calm and a great release, as if I had accepted all losses, all deaths. Moll was there. Belle was there. Better, I was there. I was I, for the first time. I breathed in joyously the hard sweetness of the licorice and tobacco in the air.

CHAPTER 9

Three days later, I met the minister, Henry Davis, slipping, like a crow along the icy road. His long white hair and rose cheeks brightened by his black buckram. Behind him walked Belle and a cured Neil. I braced for a lecture on my witchery.

"'Day, reverend!" I growled, "Why so rushy?"

"Another shipwreck!" He blurted, eyeing me narrowly as he slipped by on the snow. He avoided his wife's glance.

It began to snow us blind. Whatever the cause, it fit my chance exactly. No matter what the Harbor would do to me, I had to go, while my spells worked. We three scrambled after Henry, me limping in the rear on my glassy legs, repicturing Neil's rise from the grave.

Once I stopped and rubbed henbane on my aching calves.

But it did no damn good.

Through the squall, we sludged the mile to the Harbor Village. The wet snow slapped hard against us from the southeast. We got to the whitened stands of pitch pine along the Salem Road south of the Harbor. A crowd had gathered. The snow crisscrossed so thickly that we couldn't see the rock of Norman's Woe barely ten rods off the coast. All we could make out was a raft of minister gulls bobbing and weltering in the high sea. Snowflakes vanished before reaching the water, melting in the darkened air, and the waves spumed surf above the rocks, like hay being tossed into a loft. When the wind and snow relented, a brig with the signboard, "Rebecca Ann," appeared, like some mastodon fallen on its side, choking in an avalanche of wet snow. Both masts were broken off, and the ship was being riven against the rocks by wind and the incoming tide. The ship had struck Norman's Woe, invisible in high water. Screams came from the ship, but the on-shore wind obliterated our shouts of consolation.

"In the water," Neil yelled.

Yellowish white bodies rode the surf and slammed against the cliff. Halyards wrapped around the shoulders of some of the dead, as they were washed from the rocks.

I knew of a nearby fisherman's hut and went inside and found an old halyard which I anointed with Jude's henbane for luck. I returned and climbed a little way down the eighty foot cliff to a narrow ledge jutting over the water. I tied a loop, threaded it, and shot four casts that immediately brought in four bodies, as if they were blackfish. I was a fisher of dead men.

A line of people had formed above me to pass up the corpses I sent up the cliff.

"Lucky casts," said someone above me.

I craned up. It was the redheaded boy and Roger from the Gloucester Bank. They were smoking cigars of corn silk and chocolate, the kind kids wrap themselves, and the ashes dropped down their clothes. They were intoxicated by alcohol.

Red continued, "The Dogtown witches're here, don't ya know?

THE LAST WITCH OF DOGTOWN   45

Like her!" He nodded back at Belle somewhere out of my sight. Henry stood beside them, listening and worrying and accepting it all, like the coward he was.

Roger said, "We'll have to go up and help them move out of there one of these days." He almost fell and knocked Red down the cliff.

"They say they sleep in snow up there and don't feel nothin,'" He added.

I wanted to swing the halyard and sweep them off the cliff.

Red went on, "They probably sent the storm, Roger. They got storm-senders up there, that's what they got."

A narrow man angled between the two boys, looking like the Grim Reaper himself. It was Reverend Hammett, minister of First Parish. I waited for him to denounce and fine them, but he edged past to talk to Henry instead. Henry then marched down to me. He needed Hammett's influence in the Church so that our meeting-house would not be closed with the diminished population of "Dogtown."

When he reached me, he yelled, a little too loud even for the storm: "Granther, let someone else throw the rope!"

I ignored him, but he kept on. I snarled, "No— why?"

Henry said nothing, till, glancing up at Hammett staring down, he hissed, "Looks like Dogtown witchery. You're creating scandal. Think what happened in Salem. Think of our village."

"Let the dead bury the dead?" I asked. He was Calvinist all over— appearance was everything and let the Devil take all.

I glimpsed Belle on the cliff watching me with pride.

"Henry!" I screamed over the storm, so all could hear, "Those sots are calling us witches and you think I'm causing fucking scandal! Are you crazy? People are dying here."

Henry reddened and turned away, squinting into the offing for a sign.

Losing control, I madly drove on: "One hint of cuckoo criticism, and we let these people die? Is your censor always right?" In my right-eous anger, I was almost forgetting the drowning. I fired the rope. Out of the corner of my eye I spotted Henry looking pleadingly up at Hammett.

"Don't they want us off the moor?" I threw at him so roughly that Henry, in panic, edged me away, as if I were madness itself. I pleaded by pointing to the bodies in the water. But finally I surrendered the rope at his feet and climbed up.

Henry hurled the halyard at the bodies, but it fell short, the rope being too bulky for him. The dead crashed against the rocks, and heads split, green brain and blood oozing through the cracks into the plunging sea.

They needed my magic now, I thought, and they shoved me away. Then I saw one of the bodies swinging an arm more deliberately than the others. It was *alive* and had one arm around a rock but each wave was sweeping it higher, so that a fast throw was needed. His eyes locked on me, as if he were destined for me to save.

"Throw it to him!" Hammett shouted at Henry.

Henry threw again, and again, and the heavy halyard fell shorter at each throw, as Henry tired. Beaten, he looked up at the mob above him on the headland, his long white hair plastered to his face by wet snow. I thought he would tumble into the frothing sea.

Before anyone could stop me, I leapt through the crowd. Henry would lose the damn halyard, as well as himself in the sea, for the rope barely made the distance anyway.

As I passed through the crowd, Hammett grabbed my arm, but I easily shook it off. Henry clearly had no luck in him, and he was wincing under Hammett. He shook with the wet and cold and exhaustion.

"Give the rope to me, you bastard," I shouted and yanked the lanyard from his hand, almost throwing him into the water. I was wild now to show the town I was good and right. The ledge was narrow, and the wet snow too slippery. Henry and I barely balanced on the edge of the rock, so Henry yielded and scrambled back up off the ledge.

I hit the man in one throw, who slipped the lasso beneath his arms and held it for life, as he let go the rock and rode the wave that swelled him over the rock. The mob fell silent. I led him between rocks like a mule, inching myself back and forth along the tiny ledge.

Then the ninth wave tore him south toward a cascading rock. I arched back hard, but I started slipping. Carefully Neil slipped down behind me, pressing himself back against the cliff face and hooping my waist with his long arms to give me leverage. The rope stiffened, and the man was suspended, at the rock several feet from his face—until he went under.

The rope held, and he came back up waving again that he was still alive.

Crack!

I flew back against Neil, my head walloped Neil's chest, as the back of Neil's head slammed the rock wall. The frayed rope had snapped. I saw the man flung against the rock, face first, on the next breaking wave, then rebounding back, legs forking in air, careening down the far side, head first—split.

Neil whispered, "You tried goddamn hard, Granther. Goddamn hard—don' forget it. Don't blame yourself none."

I looked up helpless and saw Red and Roger with a new rope, showing Reverend Hammett how it was better than the frayed one I had used.

Hopeless of another chance, I climbed up. I ran to Hammett, shouting everything at once. Pained, Hammett looked down at me, silently accusing me rightly of vanity, selfishness, disgracing the dead. It was all true.

As I went to clean and wrap the bodies with Belle, leaving the saving to others, I saw Roger stumbling down the steep cliff path.

The salt and snow raged on.

Looking upon the green faces and open mouths and rolled-back eyes of the drowned, my vanity bore in on me harder. How my hurry in not checking the rope had cost a life, how I would be proverbed for a fool, and a warlock, if they knew, how my trust in henbane killed a man. Witchery too had been defeated. Henry looked at me pitifully, though he would have thrown and broke the rope too, if he could have. Henry had that superior look my Harvard theology masters had when I was expelled and that my father had when he caught me glancing at my mother's curing books.

Scouting the coast for the dead, I drowned my shame in the search along the shore. The thrashing sea subsided. Crows swept down on the corpses in the water and helped us locate them, pecking on their backs and shoulders, till, before nightfall, eighteen bloated bodies lay there, heads battered red, in silent accusation. Belle, me, and others laid them ghastly green in the snow, beside a bonfire. We wiped them with vinegar and wrapped them in sailcloth, which made them look horribly like basking seals.

Another living man was spotted. He still hugged the top of a rock which now rose above the relenting surf. The man held on. No one dared to throw him a line, for he was secure on the rock above the tide, which was now going out, and we could afford to wait. This made me seem all the more reckless. Later he was rescued by boat.

Before I left the harbor, I went to look at the face of the dead man I had tried to save. I lifted the sailcloth and stared at him. He looked back at me with pupil-less accusing eyes. Had Roger left them open?

I heard a familiar coughing behind me.

"That's Captain Patten of Kennebunk. He was a passenger," Belle said. Her hair full of wet snow around the bonnet, beautiful even then, her face blue from the cold and her body trembling.

I said nothing, trying to keep her from getting me to talk.

But she knew what I needed and added, "Someone just identified him. He is the only one anyone knows here. He came from Lanesville originally."

"I'd rather not know," I said, closing his eyes and covering him with sailcloth.

"Granther, you did great things! You showed them how to use the rope. These men weren't meant to die. They were meant to be saved, and you tried to save them."

I looked at her hard. So, like me, she really didn't believe in Henry's Calvinist God.

Still the wind off the ocean made me shiver with cold and shame. Now more gossip would fly, and Lizzy and Scot would stay away even longer, if they came back at all.

"Don't stop, Granther, you were meant to do the work of the Lord."

Fearful of staying in the Harbor Village that night, like the others, I dragged myself back up the hill to the Commons. Not one rock was thrown at me. I wished there had been. I felt my witchery was over—dead. I would need other means to gain Lizzy and Scot back.

My dog Start found me along the road and leapt joyfully at my hand.

That night I prayed hard that I would be right with God again.

I thought too of Belle and her beautiful pale face.

CHAPTER *10*

I wrote to Lizzy and Scot, asking them to come back, but they didn't answer.

Weeks later, I saw Belle and Henry walking through "Dogtown" Square in the direction of the Harbor. She wore a bright yellow hourglass cloak, trimmed in black, and several petticoats and a black wishbone bonnet. They had clearly been sparring, crow and warbler, for neither spoke, and Belle trailed listlessly behind, while Henry strode on ahead.

I hadn't seen her since the wreck of the Rebecca Ann. As I followed the sweep of her reddish gold hair, streaked white and fanned below the bonnet across the shoulder folds of her yellow cloak, I pictured again her wide brown eyes in their slanted doe-like cases above the thick lips and fine curve of her bosom.

She had been high church, until she came under the sway of the Puritans and later John Wesley, to whose teaching she surrendered her free will to God, like a good Molinist. It was at that time that she met Henry Davis, and he became her confessor, and mastered her doctrines—and her. She was very fleshly and felt the guilt of it.

In England, her religion had been indoors and centered about the family table and the C. of E. Cathedral at Bath. Now she was a creature of the wilderness. Her sun-reddened face would have scandalized her mother or herself at a younger age. But she had seen crosses in the rocks and read in the Book of Nature signs from the Lord. As she put it, she was "born to worship." She had worshipped Henry Davis and had worshipped Abram Wharf for a fortnight but had returned to Henry. She had worshipped the stone saints on the door of Bath Cathedral and saw herself as one of the angels climbing the ladder to meet her God face to face, even if He was bodied forth in a human being—the Lord at the top of the ladder at Bath was said to wear the face of the architect himself. She would have adored Napoleon even after he had turned into the Antichrist in Russia.

Henry was soon out of sight. Looking back and seeing me, Belle lingered.

"Is Henry exorcising, today?" I asked. I crudely stared into her eyes, feeling a growing power.

She stared back. "Granther. Good day to you. Yes, Henry is sort of exorcising. Something is stirring everyone up these days," she answered, looking away.

"Witchcraft?" I asked again, teasing her to keep her attention.

"Yes, Granther. But this is not Salem Village."

"A man can get to heaven if he builds a step every day."

She pulled me up: "That was the way of that demon Blake. Better if these people don't tease themselves with spiritual matters."

She began to follow Henry but seemed to tire and stop to rest. Or did she stop for me?

"So we shouldn't help?" I asked, sharply, forgetting for a moment my humiliation in the Harbor. I picked up a stone and spun it into the path in front of her. Upon landing, it skipped forward like a frog on the packed snow. She laughed.

I said, "We helped Black Neil, didn't we?" I hurled another stone, and, as it landed, it flitted to one side. A toad. It gave me luck.

"Fighting fire with fire?" she said. "Witches are just silly, Granther."

"Silly?" The word sizzled in my mind. I was about to pick up another stone, but I didn't need any more assurances. She was making me take up the witch cause again. I *had* felt Thomazine's power, hadn't I?

"Silly?" I repeated dumbly, "Not when they believe it."

"Not when *you* believe it?" she flung at me.

Belle pulled down her wishbone bonnet over her face and buried her indignation—then laughed. She had me that time, taunting me with my failure with the drowned Captain Patten.

I walked along the Commons Road, catching imaginary flies in the cold and letting them go. Presuming her acceptance, I walked beside her.

"My mother was a healer," I reminded her.

"I had forgotten," she said and came closer. "A witch?"

"Not exactly."

She swallowed hard, and spoke with stony seriousness now. "Granther, there are things in the spiritual world that we cannot see, but they're there. Did God not make the world? It seems as natural to assume that someone, allowed by His permissive will, is out to destroy it, a Tester, by whom we must prove our virtue."

She was lost in her bonnet for a moment, then resumed: "It's not easy to renounce the Devil, and he's clever. It's characteristic of the fiend that he'd assault the woman, the weaker vessel."

I probed: "Did not God plant mysteries too in the world for us to find?"

She stopped and looked into my eyes. "I believe you're right,

Granther."

What the hell was she driving at? There was a price to pay for Belle's loyalty. Was she the Devil? Was I her witch? Was she casting off Henry? I was getting near her core somehow, and that scared me now. Here was Belle . . ..

She stopped to break off a branch of barberry by the first bars of the Commons. Looking down at the yellow buds whose flowers would later have matched her dress, she seemed to drift away again. She stayed so silently still, it seemed she did not even breathe.

Then her barberry branch trembled, and she said without looking up, "Granther, from your mother, you've some healing knowledge. I saw what happened to Neil in that awful cold." She shook the branch and stared at the closed buds without seeing them.

I felt worthy again. "Yes, I've little knowledge, yes."

"I need help, Granther," she blurted out, looking into my eyes. Then she swung away, suddenly weeping uncontrollably.

I swung her back to me. She shook me off and stepped back. "A year ago I first sensed a . . . a weakness in my chest. There was blood in my cough. No one seemed able to help. I asked Tam. She ranted and told me it was a killer baby, the Devil's child, and had to be destroyed. At the sabat, I had the cannula and trocar, for I couldn't bear the pain of children dying again. Four was enough. And the cold here and Henry's loss of favor with the new church fathers in Gloucester, blaming us for witchcraft and the rise of the new Unitarians and what else."

"And Henry's inability to fight back."

She said nothing to that. But closed her eyes and went on. "I have had pneumonia, Granther. But thank the Lord I have recovered. I asked Henry not to say anything because of possible accusations of witchcraft. But I have remained . . . weak. Yes, weakness that's the best thing to call it. The Harbor doctors can find nothing wrong now. I went to Tam. She said only the steel would help me. I remember the freezing metal passing into my . . . body. Never again! But now my weakness is worse. What can I do?"

Breaking free, I scoured the sky for those clouds, like English ships, to take me away. But blue was everywhere, no doubt melting into the seamless horizon into the sea. Why hadn't I left the village? Was I just waiting for Lizzy and Scot? Were they coming back? The only real movement was the breeze that wrinkled the cold pines like skin.

Like skin! The word thrilled me. Belle's skin. How often I had thought of it was brought home to me only now. And now, if I had power, I could save her and—? Yet the thought of forcing her to my will was hateful. I despised myself.

She went on: "The body is part of a struggle with the demons who hear triumph in the death rattle. I need help now. Perhaps Tam or you could be there. At least, I want the courage to die well. Without tears, regrets. Perhaps I will do something for you all before I die. Yes, I must *do* something before I go."

And Henry? Where is Henry in all this?

I held her to me, and she put her arms upon my shoulders, but her mind drifted away and her body was lifeless. The barberry branch fell on the snow dotted path.

Picking it up, I said, "Let's talk to Neil and Judy Rhines."

She followed without a word.

But what was I about to do? I went feelingly.

CHAPTER 11

It was early dark when we got to Judy Rhines'. In the window, we saw Jude sitting candle-lit at the puncheon table with Moll Jacobs, the daughter of the night with the fiery highlights gleaming in her curled hair, unlike Judy's untamable black wires. Black Neil was not there. Judy Rhines and Moll were passing a smoking rum mug back and forth. Mollie's cigar lay burning on the table.

I swept Belle in without knocking. Judy and Moll jumped up and hugged us. Belle offered the barberry branch with its sleeping yellow buds. Judy put it in a mason jar and sat Belle at the round table with them. Belle kept her bonnet and cloak on. I stood near the door. Judy Rhines asked, "A dram of rum?"

"No, nothing," I answered.

Belle blurted out quickly : "Judy, the weakness in my chest has not gone away." She broke into tears. My eyes filled too.

Then, laughing a horse laugh, Judy said, "A drop of smoke. Ple-e-e-ase, Belle."

She forced her to swallow a dram of hot rum. I could tell from her face that it was bitter, and it dazed her immediately. Eager for a dram now too, I now took down a good one, which Judy now handed me without asking. It had a bitter bite to it all right and made my eyes hot.

"They're smaller." Moll said, looking at Belle's cloaked bosom.

Judy Rhines snapped, "That's right, Moll. You see things invisible like that, don't you?" guffawing, showing her long fangs, like her Aunt Thomazine's.

"I knows what I knows," said Moll, yawning blearily.

Judy Rhines whinnied her horse laugh.

A dog whimpered. Spread out beneath the table was a dog, part shepherd, part wolf. It lay on straw with its mouth open in sleep, a stray I had never seen before. Its blackish hair reminded me of Judy Rhines'. Judy's guffawing had stirred it, but it did not wake.

"Elva, wake up! You're dreaming," shouted Judy, kicking it hard in the ribs. The dog rolled over on its other side.

"The Devil speaks to her in her dreams," Judy said.

"*I* don't dream," said Belle, pushing away another offer of smoking rum. We looked at her, afraid.

"Hell, you don't," Moll said. "You should listen to your dreams. Shouldn't she, Granther?" She toasted the air spirits with the mug and swallowed huge.

"But I don't dream, Moll," Belle insisted, nettled, and finger curled strands of hair.

Help her, help her!

"And you, Granther?" Judy asked.

"I dream. Yes, yes, I dream wild, wild dreams."

We all laughed.

I saw that we were to tease off Belle's negative charge of sickness;

we were drawing it into ourselves by attracting it and discharging it, like sky electricity. Our power came from the worry and fight of the victim, as if we were drawing heat from a fire. It was beautiful to do—*save her!*

"Before you go to bed, pray to God that you'll 'member your dreams, and you'll . . . ," Moll slurred, lowering her head onto the table.

"What do you know about praying, Mollie? I never seen you at meetin'," Judy boomed, and laughed and pulled up Moll's head by the ringlets. She flashed her eye teeth down in the candlelight, like a wolf herself.

Moll flung her flaming head full up and said, "That's why you're here, Belle, to see if we have some better magic than that of your old man's meeting-house." She put the cigar into her mouth and puffed hard.

Belle suddenly tucked her hair under her bonnet and said angrily, "I don't want to die, Moll."

Save her, save her!

"Of course you don't, baby," Judy said, still laughing. "Neither does Granther here."

"Open your beautiful yellow cloak and burgundy dress, Belle," said Moll, pointing to Belle's chest. I moved towards the table where they were sitting, ready to pull Belle away. Then I froze. I couldn't move, couldn't speak. Judy winked at me, but I couldn't wink back. *Christ, help—her.*

"Why? I couldn't. With Granther, here," Belle crossed her arms.

"Stays, too," Moll said, pretending to unlace herself. "Sky-clad."

"Yes, open, open, Belle," said Judy, "Granther's an old healer's son, ain't he? Let's see. We can all help cure it that way, ha-ha."

"But it's inside," Belle said, clutching at her cloak.

"It's the Devil's brand," said Judy, "outside or in."

"Yes," said Moll, shutting her eyes. "Maybe it's the Devil's child."

"It's not the Devil's mark," I wanted to say but couldn't.

"The Devil's teat," Judy said, as if she heard and contradicted me.

"Try the cold steel," slurred Moll.

"I did. Tam did," said Belle. "I couldn't again." She reached for the rum mug herself now and drank.

"That's the Devil speaking, all right," Judy said.

With tears, Belle stood and slid off her cloak and dress and opened her stays. I couldn't turn away. Moll felt Belle's chest. Then Judy massaged her breast.

"It will feel better, Belle," Judy said. "We shall all feel better."

Belle sucked in her breath, coughed, and wrenched away to a corner. To save Belle from these demons—or healers? A glamour was over me. They had the power seat—not me.

"We must look for the Devil's mark to remove the spell. Take all your glad rags off. If it's there, we can remove it, but if you're accused, they'll undress you in public and push needles into you to see if you cry out," Moll said and howled.

"That's madness," Belle said. "People don't do that any more. We think better now, thank the Lord. Even Salem recanted."

Judy Rhines said, "People do those things still, though not the same way. We must find out who belongs to the devil, right, Mollie? The body. We forget about the shit-ass body. It tells a story, a story of being taken by the Devil. It's the Devil's book, like Nature is God's Book. Ain't I a good preacher woman?" She yowled.

"Amen," Moll said, shaking off her drowse.

My feet tingled. Belle! But I still couldn't move or speak.

Quickly Belle took off her white petticoats and stood naked. She still had curves where Lizzy had angles. Her breasts, diminished or not, were beautiful to me. Slowly Moll and Judy and I examined her, like gleaners, they with their hands, I with eyes that I couldn't shut. In the candlelight, her body was bright patches and dark shadows, a winter landscape, not sagging at all with age. Moll took a long hat pin and drove it into her breast.

Belle screamed.

"It is all right, sweet Belle," Moll said.

Judy smiled, "No, the minister's wife is clean of the Devil's mark."

"I must, must go," said Belle, angrily taking a coin out of her muff to make them stop.

"But your fortune," said Moll, smearing some black salve on the wound and bandaging it with white gauze. "You want to see the future, don't you?"

Belle dressed quickly.

Then she edged back to the table, as if drawn by force. Entranced, she sat again. Judy Rhines rose and smiled gently and brought down a caddy of tea leaves. She spooned some leaves into her mouth, chewed, and spat into a tea cup. For the first time, I could move now and peered over their bowed heads but saw only Judy's wild wires.

"What do you see, Jude?" Belle asked after a moment.

"I think you can see for yourself," Judy said.

Belle took the cup in her hand and angled some candlelight into it and stared into the teacup. "Shadows of dancers," she said, "shadows of dancers."

"What else?" Judy asked, lowering her thicket of black wiry hairs and peering in.

"A man is . . . is kissing a woman," Belle said slowly.

"Who's the woman?" Judy asked, looking hard at Belle.

"I don't know," she said, avoiding Judy's eyes and staring into the cup.

"You do too," Moll snickered, peering into the cup.

"Who's the man?" Judy asked again.

I held my breath. *By God, let her live!*

"It's the Black Man," Belle said, almost breathless.

"Look again," Moll said, throwing her head back and howling.

"Who's the woman?" Judy asked again.

"Can't see," Belle shouted, shutting her eyes.

"*Who's* the man?" Moll spat out. "You know him well."

I held my breath again. I could feel my new pact with Belle die before it had begun, when they would speak my name in adultery.

Shame flooded my heart. I turned away. I wanted Lizzy back.

"It's my husband."

I breathed easy.

"Hell's bells—it is," Moll rang out. My legs exploded pinpoints of pain. Judy leapt up and flung the cup against the door beside me. It didn't break. "The sabat. Did you enjoy your sabat?' Judy asked, handing Belle the rum mug.

"I was never there," said Belle, taking a dram.

"But I saw you," Judy said. "Didn't *you*, Granther?"

"That was only tea leaves," I said, finding a voice.

"It was the next sabat," Moll said, "And you'll be there, Granther. I can see you. You're leading us now."

Before I could answer, Judy said, "More rum for the toast."

"Yes, more rum," said Belle. She looked at me. Was she intoxicated or witched?

"Yes, more rum," I said, surprised at my calmness and docility. I was making an easy pact.

Moll had fallen asleep on the table, but Judy Rhines stood and pulled her up by the elbow. She handed Moll the rum mug and me the barberry branch.

Moll slopped rum on the table as she looked at me and slurred: "Here's to Granther Halliday, King of the Witches! He will save you, Belle."

"And us," Judy Rhines answered.

I waved the barberry branch, as if in benediction, and bright drops fell on them like rain.

Belle and Judy Rhines looked at me and clapped. *Belle!*

We left. We strode quickly along the dark Back Road, and some phantom followed us. It was the wolf dog, Elva, now awake and restlessly moving across the back of our path. Many other shadows moved behind her—the pack I had seen Thomazine with that night.

"Do simples work?" Belle asked suddenly, not noticing the dogs, that had become too common now.

"Let us try it!"

"Yes, let's." she answered. "Help me, Granther."

"I shall," I said, watching the dog pack.

I kissed her hand, and she ran off, making soft crunches in the blue, moonlit snow.

Elva ran after her, circling the way wolf dogs do, but not coming near. The pack stayed far at bay. Belle was still too entranced to notice the dogs. I followed her unawares, till she barred her door.

That week the rest of the snow disappeared, and I found some plantain and gave her some leaves.

"You drink the juice for the privates," I told her.

CHAPTER *12*

My nights were restless and all too silent now, so I walked about. Only dog yowls in the dark. Cattle or rocks seemed to stir. But no wagons passed anymore, and no wagon brought back Lizzy or Scot. One night there were terrible signs.

First, I lost footing, plunging a leg up to the thigh in Granny Day's half frozen-swamp.

"Help. Help," I floundered. Or rather a voice called that was mine but wasn't. I jerked my leg out in panic. It was a thinner voice I heard. I forgot myself and rushed towards it. Lizzy?

"Hep me!"

The voice came from farther up the path to the Commons Road. The cry grew weaker as I came closer. In front of a rock were two crutches. In the dark, two red-stockinged legs stuck out from under the snowy bushes. "Hep me up," the voice whined louder. Ghost? No. It was the voice of a woman. Her head was wrapped in a black shawl so that her face could not be seen. I grabbed for her hand, but she snapped it away. I grappled it, pulled her up, and steadied her, light as snow, to her feet and slid the crutches under her armpits. Then the bonneted woman screamed an uncanny scream that I shall always hear: "Eeeeeah! He's going to kill me. He's going to kill me! Kill me!"

Dropping one crutch, she struck my cheek with the other. My head reeled. White and shaking, I let go, and the woman clumped back down into the snow, like a corn dolly.

A streaming torch came running led by a leaping dog. The man was tall and wide and still yellow-haired and straight: Abram Wharf with his Irish setter. He wore his old Continental bluecoat uniform and was staggering drunk. He often imbibed in the woods. He had started several fires, but luckily there was always water in the fire cistern to put them out.

"Easy. Easy. He does this all the time now," Abram said, shaking, giggling. "It's you, Granther. It's all right. Everything's right now. Easy, Granther, my grandfather."

Wharf swung the torch wildly toward the back of the rock. A shower of sparks made the setter leap and bark. On the ground, the shawl having fallen off, lay Sammy Stanley crying, also called Sammy Maskey, who always wore women's clothes. Sammy was dirt-poor and had turned thief. He was still yowling, "He tried to kill me!" I lost my temper. I pulled him up by the housecoat front, ready to bang his head against a rock. Here was one score I could settle. Abram saw me serious now, and he suddenly sobered. His shame stopped me. I should have known Sammy.

"Go home, Granther," Abram said.

Turning to me, he added, "Sammy's taken to doing this to folks, goin' outa his plow line—and you don't look too well yourself, my grandfather. Pay no heed to poor Sammy. Says he's been to a sabat, and

ever since, a witch has been tryin' to kill him. Says his legs got cursed
and he needs these crutches to get about and that some other witch has
to protect him. This witch business will murder this village."

"You're a young fool, Sammy." Abram spoke on. "You think witches are healers. Well, your mother gave you a fool's heart as well as
women's clothes. There ain't no witches. Are there, Granther? Just
murderesses who murder their darlings." Wharf laughed and swayed
his torch and laughed again, a light, low laugh, that sputtered into a
cough and added, "That's all dafftness."

"No, no such thing," I said, and he started to shuffle home
through the snow.

"Go home, Sammy boy," Abram called after him, shaking his torch
so wildly with laughter I thought the fire would rain down on his head.

Abram Wharf would have been a good ally in witchery, if he
weren't so dead set against it, for he had a boldness about him, though
it could be dangerous, as when he charged into The Gloucester Bank
with his dueling pistol. Old as he was, he had helped me raise my
Boo—I did still owe him the two dollars—and we hunted stone marten
together. Ever cheerful, he bore things lightly, often too lightly, like his
way, old as he was, with the wives of others.

"Come, Sammy, I'll help you home," Abram said, following and
reaching out a shaking hand in the darkness toward Sammy. Then,
without either saying another word, they stumbled off down the
"Dogtown Road," like a shaky pillar of fire, into the snowy night.

I couldn't face the empty cabin any more, so I went back to the Boo.

There I lit a candle and looked up into the darkness inside the tur-
reted roof. It had cathedral depths tonight. Wharf and I had built it up
of slabs and turf, buttressing it hard against a great boulder, and we put
on the conical turret roof. Embarrassed by this extravagance, I just
slapped tar paper on the roof and never did paint it, just put on linseed
oil on the rest and it weathered the snow rot. It was a small folly, called
the "witch's hat" by Abram. Red must have been a seer, when he said
"witch's den." I slept there that night and dreamed of teeth.

The next day, Abram Wharf came to the Boo. The snow had turned to fog.

"Morning, General Wharf," I said.

Abram's large frame filled the doorway like a plowhorse. But he did not laugh as usual.

"Morning, Granther."

He did not look up, as if he feared the evil eye, but stared at his hobnails, which I had mended. It was alarming. Abram was always sunny. Now he was the fog itself. And sober. He did not even shake.

"Get Cropper and we'll go hunting, fog and all," I said.

"Ain't got no dog now," Abram said, staring up into the dark shaft of the Boo tower.

I diverted him: "Raised the roof well, didn't we, Abram? Thanks to your sure eye, the witch's hat went on," I said. But Abram cracked no smile. Fearing what was afoot, I went on, "Don't fret. I've your money for you." I hadn't thought to give him the money but something made me say it. Abram said nothing.

"Sit down," I said. "I've stoked the fire." I hadn't, but now I hurried to do it.

Abram sat slowly down in the peasant chair. He grew calm.

"Now where's Cropper?" I asked.

"Had to shoot Cropper this morning. Turned crazy, like the other dogs. Dunno how I did it."

"Witchcraft?" I blurted out like the village fool without thinking.

"Oh, plenty girls for witchcraft in the village. No, no. Cropper must have gone bad like the whole damned village. He was drooling and biting and all." He started to laugh.

"Too bad. Those stone martens will be glad," I said, forcing a smile.

"Huntin's over for me."

"Nonsense, Abram. We'll just take Start."

"Sure," he said, "We'll just take Start." He stared at the bucket of cold, dirty bees wax and pitch on the floor and coughed nervously.

"Granther," he said, "Could I use your whetstone?"

"Sure."

I brought it down from a shelf and poured whale oil on it. Abram flicked a pearl-inlaid razor from his boot. He opened it, took the stone, and began whetting, making deep fishhooks scars on the oilstone.

"Beautiful aren't they? I mean the rainbows on the steel."

"Where did you get that cutter?" I asked.

"Found it under my old house."

The carven stag peered over his bent shoulder alarmed. There was a dead-fish look to Abram's eye. It made my voice creak. I asked, "Why ruin your foot and your boot carrying that?"

"A great joker you are, Granther. Ruin my foot and boot! Ha-ha." He laughed too hard, then simpered. He studied his hobnailed infantry boots, the leather dried and worn to the color of potatoes, but my soles and heels still held. I wanted to console Abram for Cropper, but no words came. I didn't have them. I moved closer to grab the razor from him.

Abram eyed the blade edge: "Granther, you think people who kill themselves go to heaven?"

"How the blazes should I know? But I hope you never do anything like that, Abram Wharf. Why should you? It's wasteful. Yes, you go to hell you do that."

"That's what my sister said. *Wasteful.* 'Waste not, want not.'"

He seemed asleep, but suddenly shouted at the ceiling: "Why the fuck should we endure it here?"

"Because where's there's life, there's hope, you old fool." Even to myself, I sounded hollow as Rafe's Crack, but I couldn't stand anyone gnawing on himself like that.

Abram chuckled low: "Do tell, Granther. Do tell."

"Look, the village is rotting like an old schooner, so? Go to the Harbor Settlement. Go to sea. Go."

"You stay, Granther."

"I stay," I admitted. Then I lied: "I'm working on some plan that may help us." I must go after Lizzy and Scot.

"Bright ideas ain't so bright anymore, Granther. Even if you got 'em." Abram coughed slightly and began to wave the open razor about, slicing the air, as if he were cutting down a dressed skin.

To distract him, with an awl I marked out a piece of leather for a last and asked him casually, "Abram, lend me your razor, a moment, please."

"No, Granther. Need it." He snapped away from me quickly.

I lunged for the razor and caught the blade as he swung it up and held on. He twisted it in my hand , and it rode hard into my palm. At the sight of the ribbons of blood streaming out from between my fingers, Abram let go.

I stanched the cut with a shoe rag. Then I folded the blade and put it on a shelf behind me.

"Sorry, Granther. You jumped me a moment." Abram laughed low and stared at my throbbing hand wrapped in the bloody rag. I longed to hold Abram's head in the bucket of cobbler's wax.

"If I were you, I'd go home now," I said.

"Yes, yes," Abram said, smiling profusely. "Home is where I'm agoin'."

But he remained sitting.

Then I looked again in the fish eye and said, "Wait. Here's the two dollars for the raising, if you don't mind my blood." I added, "You think that's enough, don't you? Don't get above your raising."

Abram didn't laugh, just gawked out the window behind the Boo. I slipped the full two dollars in coin into his pocket. With a sudden wrench, Abram pulled himself up and yanked open the door and hurled himself out the doorway, as if it might trap him.

From the window, I watched him close himself in the foggy

Commons Road. When the blood sopped through, I rebandaged my hand. I waited for the little custom there might be, waited for the world to call—hadn't this always been my lot? Why *didn't* I bring back Lizzy and Scot at gunpoint? Instead I put the wax on the stove and heated it. I stirred it vigorously with a stick.

A half hour passed. The stag on the peasant chair stared and questioned and made me feel useless and queasy. Divinations flashed. I *knew* Abram was dead! I ignored them, watching the bubbling wax. Then a furious slapping and crying on the door told me what I already knew had happened.

I held the door handle a moment. Then I tore it open. Sammy Maskey stood there on his crutches, his face shadowed deep inside his wishbone bonnet: "Abram has cut his own throat with a razor! Quick! Come! Granthers, please come! The bright blood!"

We ran down The Commons Road. As soon as we turned toward The Commons Square, there under a rock with a blood cross on it lay Abram Wharf, face up in the snow under the same rock where I had found Sammy. The razor in his hand was mate to the one I snatched from him. Abram had marked a cross with his own blood on the rock. The wound in his throat gaped like a great mocking smile that said: What did you do to save me, Granther?

For a moment I wished I *had* killed him, the way Abram threw his life away against mine, as if I were God and could have preserved him. Perhaps in my mind, I did kill him, killing him with my curses, my neglect, my not searching his other boot for the matching razor. I was the village idiot again. Abram died in front of me. And I thought of saving the Settlement?

I looked at Sammy who had pulled deep into the dark of his wishbone bonnet. I fished into Abram's pocket. The coins were gone. I stood in front of Sammy. He took out the coins from somewhere in his skirt and gave them to me.

"I couldn't have killed him," Sammy said.

It was true.

I kept the coins to give to Abram's sister. I looked so angrily at Sammy that he slunk off. I stared down at Abram. "What should I have done?" rang in my head.

Always the past tense.

CHAPTER 13

Abram was buried where he died, and the road named after him in compensation for his missing grave marker. That very day of the funeral, I was watching out the window of my Boo and planning my visit to Haverhill to explain to Lizzy our exit from the village to Gloucester Harbor, when I saw Sammy Maskey leave a book on my doorstone. I saw his wishbone bonnet through the window and called to him, but he ran off, limping but crutchless.

The book turned out to be the *Malleus Malificarum,* "*The Hammer of Witches.*" No doubt Sammy brought it on orders from Thomazine because I was the new king of the witches or whatever nonsense she was cooking up. I had enough Latin left over from Harvard College to read it slowly. At first, as I read it, I thought it was sent by

Belle or the Reverend Henry Davis to *dissuade* me from witchcraft, since it was an attack on witchcraft by the Dominican Inquisition. But, as I read on, I learned how this book taught more witchcraft than it scared away. Written by Fathers Kramer and Sprenger over four hundred years ago, older than *The Book of Common Prayer* itself, it charmed me now that witchcraft was presumed dead in the world. We live in the Age of Reason and of Hope and Progress. But it had something we had forgotten. Not that I half believed its lurid stories, but those two old blackfriars showed me that it is not what cures you believe in that count, but what cures you can make others swallow. Thomazine's gospel. Moreover, if there were no real witches, that was no reason that there couldn't be witchcraft. A false doctrine I learned is just as good as a true one, if there is a true one, for all my beliefs were being sorely tested now. But such views were dangerous in New England where freedom often got the gibbet or at the least a flung stone.

Thomazine had been the only one hereabouts to prosper, but now her powers were waning. If she could not bring Judy Rhines back, the more I read the book, the more I became convinced that I could bring *my* family back and revive the village. Abram had died because he could not believe in the spirit, of which witchcraft is but one form.

I experimented. Black Neil had trouble with those horse teeth of his. At Judy Rhines', I brought out some lead, heated it, and held it over Neil's head in a bowl of water. It congealed into a cloud formation of Thomazine's face. I told Neil that his sickness was caused by Thomazine's black charms. But Neil suspected it anyway; he had seen such voodoo in Louisiana where pain opens up the spirit's eyes.

I suspected all the villagers had a capacity to feel witchcraft, especially since the Universalists were conquering the Calvinists, and religious doubt was in the air. When free will and salvation for all were stripping people of their beliefs, not to say their consciences, their hearts needed release. Now minds floated, not knowing what to believe. Ideas like this could make you mad if you worried about them too much, that made my father keep speculation down by always taking inventory of his iron-mongering shop in the Old Country.

It was easy now to follow on the history of superstitions that emanated from our strange village. If our old Luce George had taught Thomazine, and she did, if Thomazine and all others told fortunes and Moll at her age still cast a glamour over men and Judy Rhines had enraptured Black Neil, if the minister's wife would resort to black arts to save herself—well, if I still had more doubts, they were soon violently dispelled.

. . .

One Saturday morning, invigorated by a sense of my new powers, I wandered out of my Boo. Some spirit led me to Eastern Point where I scouted about Fresh Pond near Brace's Cove, where an old witch Peg Wesson long ago had her kucking. Perhaps witches commemorate that event, with or without Satan presiding. Sure enough the ground was blighted. Toads were everywhere—a sign—though preposterous. I had read in the *Malleus* that after the initiation ceremony and the testifying, the witches bragged about their deviltries or got flogged by scorpion whips for doing no mischief and the toads danced and the witches promised to bring them infant blood. I was not such a hayseed to believe all that, but still there might be something in it. The witches might pretend that the toads heard them, while the witches were only cementing their own pact, whether or not a Satan or his stagman were present.

The warm mud of mid March sank deep, and the roads were impassable even for a light cart. Rain had saturated the paths around Fresh Pond, and salt competed with the smell of skunk cabbage in the air. I could see the cups of the pitcher plants full with early insect corpses, like the bodies of babies drowned in a pond where no God could save them. There grew the mayflower, the promise of spring, its flowers looking deceptively like the drops of snow it replaced. It might have been 1619, a year before the pilgrims set up their village.

Voices. Laughter. I moved closer.

A flash! A fist in the eye! A mime in a true dream!

But it was there: the sky was on the ground: Moll was lying on the grass on her blue cape with her skirts up, laughing. Reverend Davis was standing over her, like a stag. Then he was unbuttoning himself and getting on top of her. Laughing, he signaled to her to be quiet by raising his finger to her mouth. She pursed her lips lewdly in reply and grabbed his member. "More," Moll laughed and recklessly called out, "More, more." Moll lunged upward, as if trying to levitate them both into the air, as if they had annihilated each other into a single animal being.

Then all was quiet, except for Moll's gurgles of laughter.

Henry lay beside her and gazed up at the sky, till Moll massaged him again and he went back on her with even more drive. I saw now how much Moll looked like Belle. I stood stunned, like an ox about to be butchered. I couldn't think. Pines swayed in the light breeze, and the distant ocean froze to immutable, gray stone. Henry was bewitched, something had taken its course, some chemical, some drug, some spell had been cast on the village. We were lost. Moll, Thomazine, Judy were taking possession. And I saw all this coming.

I was now clammy with fear and joy, erect myself, while I walked back by Wonson's Farm, from where I could see Ten-Pound-Island Light of the Harbor Village. A four-masted Swedish bark rested in the harbor, its lifeboat lying like a cradle or a coffin in the davits and holding a yellow retriever like Start. The dog hung its muzzle between its paws over the gunwale, ears down, enjoying the sun without thoughts of its feral cousins in the woods around the Commons. Sailors were untying the sheets, for the ship was about to sail. The canvases fluttered like giant swans before they were reefed. I suddenly envied the dog its peace and its future. I thought of escaping to the Banks, then to Oslo, and back to England. But could I draw Lizzy back? Would she come after me? Rather than escape I would trust to some powerful magic, like what drew Henry Davis to Moll Jacobs and Belle once to Abram Wharf. Things were breaking apart like ship's planking. Someone had to stay and lead and restore. *The Malleus!* The witchery that once scared the world! It was still in us, covered over with the clothes of civilization. I was on my own soul voyage now. Men need masters to love or to hate—or all is lost. How to command the boys fishing off the quays, workers fleshing the skeletal hulls of boats with steam-curved planking. How to command the wives with their farm produce bargaining for fish in Billingsgate language. How to seduce a minister. That knowledge was power. Most of all it would bring Lizzy back and Scot. But was Belle too not within my sights now? Rulers always had mistresses. I would command myself best in order to command others.

I came to the rocks and trees of Dogtown. All was changed, revealed. Among the scattered trees draped in spring yellow, the moor rocks were like the building blocks of a great castle that lay waiting to be created. Civilization proper had never come to Dogtown. It was all delusion—till now. Even a hundred years of oxen couldn't drag away all the boulders, so the biggest stayed. The Dogtown world was inverted: the rocks were bigger than the trees. We were cast back on ancient superstitions. Here was the mill for witchery, whose stony head I saw coming out of the womb. Without realizing how fast I had traveled or what paths I had followed, I paused and realized that I was indeed looking through the yellow woods at the great split rock of Whale's Jaw, breaching the earth like a great, fertilizing, stone fish. The meaning of Dogtown was now to be invented in the way the *Hammer of Witches* showed, without meaning to, that witchcraft was always re-invented.

CHAPTER *14*

That I was receiving the wand of witchcraft was further reinforced that Friday night when I returned late from mailing another letter to Lizzy and Scot. I thought now, not of our quarrels about witchery that were so full of hate, but again of those times we had at corn huskings and at blueberrying in Briar Swamp, when Scot would bring along the half-mad Allison Millet. Those days before the village itself took sick.

It was close to midnight, and I was lost in such thoughts. I had had some brew at Philemon's Tavern and had been challenging the wits of the wet-noses there.

Just before I reached Thomazine's house, she swung out onto the road ahead of me and hobbled up Fox Hill faster than anyone could go and went down the moonlit trail between the boulders towards the Commons Square.

I followed but soon lost her. At the crossroads in the square, I could hear her gurgling her flask of dire and cursing and crying out about Judy Rhines in her sobby way.

Then I thought I was having visions.

Slowly, without difficulty, she crawled up a rock above Granny Day's swamp. I never thought she could do it, old as she was. It must have been the help of the Devil that raised her to the top of the rock. She stood up, looking like a gull from hell, her housecoat flapping in the light moonlit breeze. She threw her leather bottle away. She looked towards me, as if she knew I was there in the dark trees behind her, but she could not have seen me with any mortal sight. I awaited her conjuring and her throwing her arms out to each of the eight directions.

A wave fluttered and thundered through the moonlight.

She was gone.

She had hurled herself into the icy swamp! My legs turned glass with pain again.

I heard screaming—she was still alive! I stumbled towards her through the dark bushes and sucking water, slicing my face on the thorny brush, trying to heave her out by her arm, my foot swallowed by soft mud.

I snatched sapling branches. They broke off. I tried swimming. I got tangled in the brush. Spouting, becoming delirious, I sank deeper. Choking, I fainted and came to and thrashed and swam in place, until my foot hit some submerged tree trunks.

They held.

I edged toward her, keeping an uneasy foothold on the logs. I touched her shoulder, and she began to sink, face down. Gripping her wools, I slid her carefully behind me, so that I got in front of her. I pushed her backwards by her shoulders, stopping to lift her head above water for a moment, before pushing her farther, trying to keep her face above water. As soon as I smelled the dire, she started to vomit. It spread on the water like moonlight. A rotted log crumbled, and I couldn't set my foot.

We went down.

I floated myself up, but I had no footing. She was dying. I knew that. I could hear her choking rasp. I grabbed her again. But her heavy bulk of water-logged skirts and shawls slipped from my grasp. I was screaming like a baby, watching her drown. Captain Patten's arm waved in front of me and Abram's cut throat.

Then a log nuzzled my hand. I snatched it and pressed it down with my knee and put it beneath her lengthwise. I floated Thomazine precariously up, barely balancing her face on the log's end. I slowly backed her to the shore.

"Easy, Granther."

It was Black Neil.

I floated her a foot or two closer to shore. Then Thomazine rolled off and sank. But Neil reached her feet and pulled her quickly to shore.

A sopping mass of wool, she lay on the cold ground. Neil respirated her by rhythmically pressing her upper back, and she regurgitated foul water. Soon her mumbled cursing told us that she was far from dead.

As Neil got up, she rolled and swung her arm like a bat and clouted Neil. The blow knocked him into a thicket. I twisted her arm, and her, back to the ground. But the Devil had made her strong; she wrenched about like a blackfish, even when I sat on her back. She was insensitive to pain.

She shrieked, "Drown. Drown. Wanted to drown!" Neil pressed down her face into the mud. I thought of kicking her, her howling like a soul in Hell already.

Neil said, "Maybe she ain't done the Devil's work somehow, and he's apunishing her. Perhaps God wants her now, and it would be wrong to hold her back from death."

"Get Jude!" I cried.

Neil ran.

She calmed. I was doing Thomazine's will: bringing Jude back. Her witch luck!

"Judy's coming," I shouted. "Quit, Thomazine."

After a few moments, she began to shriek again. To quiet her, I stretched out on top of her, covering her with my body. Giving up, she whimpered. Then she choked. I pressed my mouth on hers and breathed her, letting her exhale. Her nose was bleeding, while my own face, cut by brambles, was bleeding too. Our blood blended. Finally she breathed lighter.

When Neil and Judy arrived, Judy put some salve up Thomazine's nose, and the bleeding stopped altogether. Then she gently put some on my sliced cheek.

Judy Rhines said, "Granther, the old bank pirate has sent us a letter, saying that our land isn't ours. A new survey claims Tam and I live on land owned by the bank 'cause of an old unpaid loan."

"But Luce George was there a century ago."

"You telling me?" she said.

"Where will we go when they drive us all out?" I asked.

"Dunno, Granther, but you boys better do something about it," Judy Rhines said, whinnying her horrid laughter. Then she and Neil took Thomazine back to Neil's house in the Commons Road nearby.

I had saved a witch from drowning, and I had completed my pact with Thomazine by re-uniting her to her niece. I was near the peak of my powers. But Thomazine's fall from the precipice was a warning to me.

CHAPTER *15*

Haverhill. 18 March 1830

Dear Granther,

For my part, I am willing in the light of God and in the council of my family to rethink my duty as a wife, as I hope that you shall, as a husband, reconsider our Christian marriage and do nothing that is untoward that bond. Word soon.

Your affectionate wife,
Elizabeth.

P.S. I hope that you shall not shame us, father.

Your dutiful son, Scot.

That was all. All! In my pride, I could not beg her. She didn't write again.

No cobbling, no tooth-pulling—business moribund, I could only watch the slow unbuilding of the village, the return to sea gulls and dust. Already the many torn and gutted houses had sweet fern and bayberry blanketing their splitting foundations. Granite blocks fell into the cellar pits and looked like the broken-open graves in the Last Judgment illustrations. Villagers sold out and left for the sea, the Harbor, the poorhouse. Animals died, except the dogs. And my wearied mind turned back to magic sure as a compass needle. Barely twenty houses were inhabited, or even standing, for the lumber of abandoned houses was all taken in the Harbor to build the new ones. Cattle and more cattle grazed on the moorland. But the land owned me now. The bank, the Harbor Village, Lizzie's family, everything had become alien, but the ugly, rocky moor of Dogtown Commons. At Harvard College, even in Dartmouth prison during the `12 War, I could not change my ways.

In early April, the dogwood raised its tiny windmill of sails, and the magnolia burst like popped corn. It was warmer than usual, as if compensating for the late, cold winter, and the viburnum already gave off its reek of lusty perfume. The dandelions, or shit-a-beds, as we called them, were imprinting the ground, and Thomazine and others were often seen gathering their leaves. The yellow buds of swamp maple and horsechestnut seemed to feed on the salt air that blew from the southwest its comforts from below the equator.

One morning, I saw Belle picking the early dandelion greens. I watched her blue dress with black dots billow like a jib as she bent and put them into her burlap bag. Was she better? I had not seen her since I gave her the plantain and was certain that she was avoiding me.

I came up and surprised her: "Belle, I know where the greens are better."

"Granther! God has given good fare right here," she said, pushing her sunset hair from her face and holding up a fistful of greens, like Judith with the head of Holofernes. "There is abundance here, Granther. Let Moll and Judy Rhines gather them. Be sure to tell them, Granther. Henry and I have quite enough. Besides they are barely growing, poor things."

This was rotten sailing. She again seemed to have forgotten her recent intimacy with me. I was a stranger again.

"How're you feeling, Belle?"

"Fine, Granther—yourself? And your good wife?" She tapped my chest playfully with the greens.

She twitched me smartly there. Henry in between Moll's legs came into my mind's eye. As the sun struck her, I noticed a yellowish tinge to her face, even though she had been in the sun some time. My mind raced feverishly ahead: the plantain had failed and she was going to die! My mother told me once how the roots of cinquefoil boiled with vinegar cured. I had used it on Abram Wharf, who for all his swash-buckling was terrified of toothpulling. Abram who would single-hand-edly punch a ring through an ox's snout would wail like a baby when I touched one of his teeth.

"Belle, you are gathering simples and must believe that witches know other medicines than doctors."

"They're all helpers, Granther. But death has its purposes. All is for the best." She let her hand of dandelion greens fall by her side. Then added sulkily, "I *am* tired today."

I roused her to battle! "Doesn't God want us to fight the fight to live?" I raised her free hand up in the air by the wrist, as if she had just won a prize fight. She laughed. I lowered her arm but held on to her wrist.

"Somehow, yes," she said, forgetting her train of thought, her mind drifting up into the ocean of blue sky above us. Then suddenly she returned to earth with sudden resignation: "The race lives on."

"Would you try my cures again, if they might work now?" I pre-tended I was a doctor, and held her wrist to my ear and listed for her pulse, and she laughed again. But her throb was weak.

She paused, "If one didn't have to sell one's soul to the Devil first."

Black battleships of cloud cruised over the grass.

She pulled away and threw the greens down, as if she hated them. She wheeled on me: "There is a curse on this damned settlement, Granther—Damn, isn't there? Something's terribly wrong. The Indians gone—no one knows why. The village dying. The witchery of Peg Wesson and Luce George. Abram dead." She was in a fright. Here was a chance.

"Most everyone believes in witches hereabouts. You can't tell someone who has seen a witch and felt her power that there ain't none," I said, biting my upper lip, snatching up the greens with exaggerated vigor. "Not even Henry could do that."

She snapped back: "Satan has his ways to be sure. But innocent people were hanged and crushed in Salem," Belle said, refusing to take the offered posy of greens from me.

I was the Tempter in the Garden: "How do we know what powers hide in the world, in these woods, in ourselves? Maybe we deny our powers because we're terrified of them."

"But they should be powers of good, not of black magic," she snapped.

"Perhaps there's no difference."

She relented; she had no energy to resist now. Absently, she took the greens back. "Well, right now I'm bringing these greens to Tam. Perhaps you'd like to come along."

I stepped closer, and my knees popped. I did not dare look her in the eye. I was absurd, all racked with pain. Physician, heal thyself! I was hardly a fit vessel for curing but I couldn't stop. I said, "Let me try a cure. My mother's often worked in the old country."

She said nothing, tamely followed me to the Boo. I could not keep from eyeing her swaying figure, a blue sheaf tied tight about the middle, the wave of her blue dress with black spots, a field for ploughing all in itself. I listened to the rustling of the cotton, as if a hand were sliding over her legs and hissing up toward her bodice. She seemed life itself, not a diseased carcass. Beside her in my black clothes and stiff legs, I was a crow, like Henry, hopping after my pheasant, while she chatted of the harvest of salt hay that would bring in a little money.

Then she added, "I gave Thomazine some of the money to pay her bank loan."

"Pay her bank loan!" I shouted at her. "But the loan was fraudulent. No one knows anymore the origins of these deeds or surveys."

She stopped and looked at me with her yellowish face: "Sometimes we must pay anyway."

"And you'll go to heaven like a good girl."

She laughed and coughed.

"Has Judy come back to Tam?" she asked, pretending not to notice her own coughing.

"Yes, they're reconciled now," I said, feeling again my godlike power.

Then I saw Belle's skin cross-lined and yellow, like a spider web blown tight in the sunlight. She *was* going to die!

"You need some new charm, Belle," I said, hardly knowing what I was thinking. "I'll find a fix-up for you."

"Things are connected," I continued, spouting nonsense to keep her attention. "They don't seem so, but—they are." I pointed into the moorland: "Grass sympathizes with the wind across the Commons, and the grass curves the wind, as well as the wind curves the grass to its will." All this sounded false, even to me. "The effect is tiny, but, my God, it's there. You must feel that, Belle. That your mind can work your fallen body, that your body can move the world a jot. Puny's the effect, but work the world you can, if you will. I don't mean grit your tushes, but let yourself feel the powers about you."

She looked at me with hope from my nonsense—and I suddenly believed my own words.

I recalled how my mother removed from a yeoman a curse from a society of secret archers. He had found one of their large crucifixes with an arrow through the Lord's forehead and had had bad luck ever since.

When we reached the Boo, I quickly seated Belle in the peasant chair. I made her bare her right arm and hold it up, elbow on the table. I rolled up the sleeve of her blue dress. I made motions of drawing invisible things in the air with my hands from near the surface of Belle's arm, as if I were playing a harp.

"Feel anything, Belle?" I asked, starting to feel my fingers imitating my mother's. But my motions were awkward, not under control. But I couldn't let Belle be another village casualty.

Belle slunk again into that trance of hers.

Then I felt her heat rushing into me. "I can feel the fire of your fever coming out, Belle," I said. "I really can. Can you?"

"Yes, yes," Belle said, waking suddenly. "It's coming out, Granther. I feel it." She began to jump about the stool like a girl getting braids.

She stopped: "But you . . .."

"I'm taking it in, Belle, but it won't hurt me a damned bit, I can tell you that. I learned this from my mother."

Belle shut her eyes and looked asleep and glowed pink. Her face lost the yellow skein. The lines sank down into her face like old plow lines flowering over. She was asleep. I played the air harp fiercer than ever. My heart leapt. Even if I was only putting a charm on Belle, I had some power. Some power. Things were connected, even if only a little. The world moved! I blew smoke from my mouth into the air, as if it were the released fire from Belle's body.

Then suddenly I went cold. I was vulnerable then.

"That's all I can draw now, Belle. Your heat's intense. It will take several draws."

Belle snapped awake. "I can't let you do this. It's horrible."

"Not right to live rather than die?"

I began again. And more heat bit into me from Belle's yellowness, like lust. I laughed wildly: "Mr. Morgan Halliday will save you, Belle."

I didn't want to stop. Again her heat fired my hands and shot through my whole body without burning. I was an insulated furnace slaking lust with sickness.

Belle grasped my hands in hers and stopped me.

She mooned close to my face and giggled, as if drunken, "Granther shall save us all."

Then she pulled fiercely away. "Enough! Enough, Granther!"

I was wild to go on, but I stopped, drained and exhilarated.

Belle quickly rolled down her blue sleeve with the black dots that ballooned out at the wrist and showed her white hand off. I held it for a moment, taking her pulse again.

"Perhaps, we can help you, Granther," Belle said, ashamed. "Perhaps, Lizzy will listen to us."

I felt bear-trapped. I made air harp movements to remind her I had some power—whatever it was. It was all around us in the air—reach out, believe, take!

Then wild barking exploded outside the door. I grabbed a hammer and flung myself out the door. Belle followed. Judy Rhines' Elva was flopping around like a newly landed fish in its death throes, writhing on her back in the road dirt, flinging herself and her blood about. She had been shotgunned. The rest of the pack had fled, as had the harbor hunter.

Desperately I tried to still her snarling bark. Twice she bit my fingers.

Finally Elva's head calmed to whimpering, quivering, twisting to the side. I tried to staunch with rags the dog's blood that bolted from her stomach, blood that mingled with my own from the bites, while Belle shrieked. I sent Belle inside and stilled the dog mercifully with the hammer.

Holding tears in a mumbling gibberish, I looked at the almost severed dog. All the life was washed out.

I felt myself stronger now as the angry spirit of Elva passed into me. Gloucester was declaring war. Anger was my food.

I took Belle home and went back and buried the dog.

When I arrived at the Boo next day, Thomazine's own Black Book of spells appeared on my cobbler's bench. The man-witch was on his own.

CHAPTER *16*

Elva's death prompted me to organize the dogs as a force for protecting the Settlement. Hadn't Thomazine some such power that night on the moor? Many dogs joined the pack now, even my dog Start. To lure him back, I laid scraps outside the Boo door at night, and the next day they were gone. The following night, I did the same. Soon I found a black wolfhound milling around my Boo and decided to train him. Neil told me he was the one that had torn his cheek in the Lurvey cellar. I was afraid the dog was blood-mad, but Neil reassured me that, since the dog was tame not long ago, I would have no trouble re-taming him. This turned out so. Though no purebred, it was a mongrel used to the gun. A recent bite on his dewlap showed his life in the wild and that promised well.

At great sacrifice, I fed him deer meat that a customer brought me for payment for keeping him in soles, while I ate cabbage soup. The dog snapped wildly when I pulled his meat away but gradually yielded to me, though to no one else. I hung a leather strip that I awled and tied to a low tree branch and let Abaijah, which was the name I gave him, flay it to bits, so he would attack any strange shoe that entered. At first, Abaijah yowled at night in answer to the dogs around the Commons, but my fat feeding paid off. On our walks, the wolfhound sprang all sorts of game I did not know were still there: hare, rabbit, squirrel, muskrat, and turkey. His presence made me feel more powerful and protected me from dogs and people alike. When Sammy Maskey came to see how I fared in witchcraft, I watched from my window how Abaijah drove him away from the Boo. When a pack of dogs appeared, I let Abaijah challenge the leader, a feisty red setter, like Abraham's dead Cropper, who threw herself against him. But the setter was so wild it took to harassing Abaijah continually, and finally, after a terrible fight, Abaijah killed her and the rest of the pack obeyed Abaijah.

Guarded from interference by Abaijah and her pack, I studied the new *grimoire* or Black Book I got from Thomazine Younger. The grimoire was bound in wooden covers and heavy metal clasps. I hadn't seen one since my mother's, which perished when our house in Lancaster was burned down by that vengeful yeoman who was under the curse of the archers. His wife had died, after my mother treated her. My mother told the man his wife was incurable.

The signs on the cover of The Black Book were the sort that I had seen freemasons use, and I laughed when he saw the author was King Solomon himself. But Sammy assured me that Solomon might very well have composed such a book. Pretending to be bent over my pegging jack, I put the book on my bench and bar-bolted the door of the Boo. I did not let in much light through the oil paper, just enough to read. My eyes were getting squinchy, especially with small, scrolled black letter on brittle paper blotted with yellow acid. It was like reading in the outhouse, the place being so small, but the book cast its spell and conquered time itself by occupying the idle hours. The admonition to celibacy was the only part that chilled me.

I learned that, if love was the power of attraction, fear was the opposite. But fear was the means of control that the Black Book recommended. All creation, sentient and inanimate, was sensitive to dread, even plants and rocks. All things were alive and shared, if imperceptibly, such feelings. The right words, could they not strike fear or love or laughter or lust? Start a revolution in the Colonies? Could not Lizzy be brought down by the right word and the right spell, so that she would say with the Black Book:

> Torture me no more. Speak: What do you
> want my hands to do?

The book would protect me:

> Jupiter's Third Pentacle fends and protects
> the callers of spirits. When the spirits come,
> hold up the pentacle, and they must do as
> you will.

Those pentacles had yet to be made and tested. A long bet, but what was prayer doing? Wasn't prayer a spell, a compulsion? And wasn't Calvin's grace further away from this certain knowledge? Wasn't virtue in:

> Go armed with fearlessness.

The secrets of understanding others were here. Neil:

> Out of work and poor, the sorcerer burns
> to find treasure in the ground. But he is
> mistaken. The gnomes of the earth hold
> their riches fast.

Moll and Henry:

> *The venom contained in the bodie of a*
> *prostitute is held in great admiration:*
> *her eye infects, entices, and bewitches*
> *many times. Her tongue, her gesture,*
> *her mien, her beauty, her impudence*
> *allure and intoxicate the mind.*

I made my own pentacles from hints in The Black Book. Conquering magic was like conquering a new continent: boldness and ingenuity did the trick. Bent over my little bench, I cut a circlet of leather fifteen inches in diameter and routed out a circle of power around the inside, an inch from the edge. In it I placed a triangle and copied the snakelike, mystic Hebrew letters, which I could not comprehend, but which promised the power of the planet Saturn to bring death, destruction, and ruin. Could I not cast these spells against Gloucester and save the village? Throw the new road somewhere else and bring back traffic to the Commons? The Universalists were now showing that free will was a power kept in harness by Calvin and Knox, who wished to check the wild horses of the populace. My Hebrew verse was Psalm 109, 17:

> *As he loved cursing,*
> *so let it come unto him:*
> *as he delighted not in blessing,*
> *so let it be far from him.*

Courage! But self-doubts ensnared me. Perhaps Thomazine's magic was superior to mine. Perhaps I would lose my soul to the Devil, if I had not already done that by being initiated—if there were a Devil! Would I be drowned by the village rowdies? Shot like Elva? If I were wrong in all this, could I shame the Devil at the last moment and save my soul?

I hove all doubt aside. I removed the horseshoe from over the inside doorway in the Boo and nailed up a pentacle, telling my suspicious customers that it was a lightning hex; anyone who knew what it was would become my ally. I was not the seventh son of a seventh son, but I knew now I had powers to cure. Had I not often cured abscessed teeth? So couldn't a curse be taken off by scratching with a pin the witch who put it on? And didn't witches inspire love as well as destroy life, reason, and property?

Fire broke out when lightning struck a black oak behind the Boo. By the time it had spread along the Commons Road, the villagers had all they could do to could keep it from the houses. The woods being overly dry that year, it gashed its yellow swath through the night woods in spite of the rain. In the flames I saw faces I had never dreamed in any hearth: hooked noses and pointed jaws of women at the stake silently shrieking, as if, like salamanders, they still lived in the element they died in. I smelled the wet stink of charred wood as I hurried through the dark smoke to the Boo to see if it had been destroyed. It was scarred by flames—an omen that it was dangerous to go on.

To batter down my fears, I went recklessly to try myself further, as the Pennsylvania Dutch children do, to see if I could powwow. I began with footsores. I would send such plagues, then heal by faith, pretending to heal by medicine. Gradually signs showed me I could control an iota of the world. Sometimes heels twisted off boots, although I fastened the pegs tight. I wished some farmer's cow dead and read it in the new newspaper, the *Telegraph*.

I killed off the more vicious dogs that were gathering about the Settlement, sending in, through my mind, Abaijah and his pack of hell hounds. I brought in a school of blackfish upon Eastern Point for village food and food for my dogs. Out of pure mischief, I caused so many pins to fall out of ladies' clothing that they began to sew more. Out of guilt, I became morbidly afraid of disease myself, since I inflicted agues of triumph on Thomazine and feared she might retaliate. I kept powdered toad in a sachet around my neck. The toad could drink in poison, the way my black buckram clothes drank in the powers about me, the way I drew off Belle's sickly heat. I believe only the toad amulet kept me free of sickness and worry about Lizzy's return then. The toad could kill the power of the spider and that was the only way to survive the village's collapse and diseases. I also carried wrapped in paper three private hairs from Moll Jacobs that she sold me for a dollar and were supposed to procure any woman I wanted.

Though I got even fewer calls to pull teeth, villagers showed a new deference to me. Sammy Maskey warned people about my powers. Though they wouldn't have admitted it, neighbors feared me, a fear of difference that I could exploit. I became reluctantly revered. "Granther Halliday is now a witch"—the word, at first joking, had spread even to the wet-noses who spent all day at Philemon's Tavern pulling at rum mugs. The old witchery was still as potent, even when mocked, as it was in the old Salem days. When a sailor fell from the rigging and drowned, I was respectfully questioned by the constable.

Constable Call's visit reminded me of the bank's treatment of Thomazine and Judy Rhines, so I sang a spell on that steel-haired president. Sure enough not long after, I saw in the *Telegraph* an article about the old pirate at the Gloucester Bank that began:

Epes Wilson is guilty of murder.

With a shock, I read that Wilson had returned from a fishing voyage to find his house locked and his young wife away at a muster in Boston. Bringing Abram Wharf's dueling pistol along, he waited for the stage. When his wife, Emily, stepped off the stage, he drew the pistol and shot her twice, once in the heart and once in the neck. In spite of Emily's scandalous reputation, he was convicted and hanged.

I was all-powerful.

There was now only me.

CHAPTER 17

While sickness drained the village energy, the dogs flourished. They would break through the Commons fences easily and run each other around the lurching oxen and cows. Rather than oversee children on the village green, as the ancients did in the Old Country, we would now watch the dogs and wish for their endurance. Neil would try in vain to get us to bet on who would appear first on an evening: retriever or lurcher, whippet or sheep dog. Their numbers and force were alarming, but they were a comforting sign of life to us who were fading, bleaching out with age too soon and with illness and dust. After someone would move off or die and his cottage caved in and was quarried, the dogs would have large litters in the potato pits beneath the floor joists. At night the feral dogs howled like wolves, echoing over the cape, warning away future settlers or telling pirates that no booty was worth the effort of a raid. Dogfights were common, and Neil called bets there too, though again there were few takers.

The dogs made some pact to entertain us. Each night at sundown, they arrived from nowhere and frisked and splashed in Granny Day's swamp, like the pupils from her old school that had closed. The dogs would drive into the swampy water and struggle, like a span of oxen trying to bolt with their 2,500 pounds of iron in tow at the new Topsfield Fair. Unlike the cattle, they could stay afloat and get out of the swamp, like some fairy race of horses that had been damned to smallness.

If the dogs were our children, they were also our guards whose large numbers, about three hundred, chased off the witch swimmers who came up drunk to the Commons. Always milling about the Commons Settlement or lying stretched their full length in the dust, the dogs lay eager and panting, till someone hurled a stick or some dog made a play bow or bit another's dewlaps. Then they flew into the swamp and out, racing to exhaustion, even death.

If the signaturists saw messages in the "writing" on plants, I might uncover some secret in the struggles of the dogs, some aid to my bid for deliverer of the village. Were not the dogs succeeding to the land, where we failed? The dogs must have some power we lacked. They were certainly better hunters and lived off the fertile rabbit and stone martin and, it must be said, off each other. If Nature is God's Second Book, then messages are written there. Familiars gave witches their insights, their force.

One sunset on the Commons, and warmer than usual, the ground fog made small, floating curtains of smoke wraiths before the dogs tilting in front of Neil and me. Neil flung a stick into the swamp: a dozen dogs flurried after, losing it among the bumping bodies, nipping at flanks, the going back awash in the tossing water, like galleons in the hate of sea fight, teeth twisted like sand sharks among dead blackfish, heads of bodiless horses—a chaos that brought home the `12 War to me.

Start was there among them. He had returned and was being coursed by my wolfhound Abaijah. I had thought him gone for good. Start plunged into the water. Renewing his energy in the swamp, he hurtled back out, but the wolfhound, keeping pace, held his bared teeth about Start's neck. Start stopped and showed surrender by baring his yellow neck to the attacker. But Abaijah tore his teeth around Start's neck in angry play before he released him. Then Start went at the bigger dog, baiting him back into the fight. The chase ragged around the houses, rocks, trees, and cloud wraiths along Wharf Road. My retriever was sliding on his side on the turns, feet still churning like eggbeaters. Other dogs joined in.

Start went down again on the ground, trampled and bitten by Abaijah. Then he scrambled up and leapt defiantly beside the wolfhound, nipping and ripping his snout, as Abaijah jabbed with his heavy head, testing for an opening. Neil threw another stick, and my retriever twisted in air but failed to catch it; it bounced off his eye, landing on the ground.

"Oaf," Neil shouted. He called on Abaijah: "Get the little prick, you hell hound. Two bits on old Abaijah, Granther."

Start shook his head, rattled his ears against the sides of his head, as if to rouse his brains, and snatched the stick with his teeth and reversed into the swamp, followed close by the wolfhound, who was a weak swimmer and was quickly outdistanced. Start led like a flagship, while all the other dogs charged after him.

Start had changed the game rules, and the other dogs now warred for mastery in the little sea of water, as they had done on land. Start had changed the rules to win. Refusing to return to shore, he swam in each direction, averting his head from all challengers, proclaiming his mastery of the water by raising his head back, the stick high in his mouth like a truncheon of authority.

Beaten now, the others retreated to solid ground, even Abaijah lay panting on the swamp edge.

"Owe me two bits," I said to Neil.

"I'll pay you, Granther," Neil said, "But them drill bits're at home. Beside you never said 'taken.'"

"That's right, you old hog slayer," I laughed. "Change the rules, like the retriever, Take the land fight to sea. The dogs are giving us a message."

"You loco, Granther?"

Start now swam to shore and dropped the stick on the ground, like an insult to the defeated Abaijah who still snapped at Start. Start darted back into the water out of reach, leaving the stick, whose attraction had now failed.

CHAPTER 18

Then I saw Belle swaying down the dark Back Road hugging a parcel wrapped in oiled paper. Puffs of mist danced around her. Her hair was fluffed out below a purple bonnet and flared like a fire, as the last of the sunset shot out under the clouds on the horizon. She wore a pale blue dress with puffed sleeves and purple trim. But even in the twilight I could make out that her face was ashen. I hadn't seen her for days and feared she was ill. She was walking slowly. She nodded at me, and I hurried away from Neil and the others to meet her.

When I came near, she brightened. "Brought some pork shoulder and potatoes. I thought with Lizzie and Scot away. . .."

"Very thoughtful, Belle. I couldn't have conjured better. Are you alone? Where is Henry?" Why was she suddenly so solicitous?

"Off to the Harbor. Business."

We dallied along towards my house, while the trees waved their arms like cheering sorcerers. I would not ask too many questions. I touched Moll's amulet of hair in my pocket. Out of the sight of others now, I took her hand. She did not pull back, but stiffened, as I leaned to kiss her, and said, "I came to warn you away from this witchery."

I guessed she was orthodox now that she was worsening. I glared at the bribe and then at the dancing trees, saying nothing. Salt was thick in the air. We stopped before my house, but when I was about to ask her in, she countered with: "Granther, Henry thinks your joking has gone too far." Then she added, "Why do you dress like a religious for all the time?"

I dropped her hand as if it were a spider and pulled her up short: "Like the minister gulls, black is natural to me. And you? Don't you think it looks well on me?"

"We think that during such poor times, one must not give occasion to scandal. And Reverend Hammett . . .."

"Ah, Most Reverend Skeleton Head."

"Granther, I know he's an ogre, but we can't be indifferent to what such persons think. People will now join the ranks of the Universalists. Certainly we can't believe that everyone is saved these days, can we? I mean some *will* be cast away."

"Like me, becoming a witch and drowning a man?"

Too hot on what she was saying, she didn't listen. Her indifference chilled my new soul, which needed nurture. And her turning on me burned deep. She said, "One can never say what the limits are to God's mercy. But the fallen are a sign to others of going too far."

I stared at the food parcel, as if it were a serpent. I recalled Belle's nipples were as large as Moll's. Were Belle's breasts now being further marred by disease? I swayed between lust and sympathy. The sorcerers in the leaves laughed in mockery.

"It's superstition," she said. "We can't afford to be superstitious now." She was hugging the bag against her light blue dress, as if it were a child. I took the bundle from her.

"Is Henry's position as minister threatened?"

"Henry is deeply concerned." The sun was just setting and made an aureole around her.

"And Most Reverend."

"And Reverend Hammett."

"And Most Reverend wants a list of the unorthodox."

She went on, "Well, Hammett is very powerful in the Harbor Village. You yourself can't drive wagons there anymore. Scandal is cursing the Settlement. Why not just stop this nonsense before scandal touches us all—God damn it, Granther!"

"Witches have always been here and everywhere, seen or hidden—everywhere and for a reason!"

"Disobedience. That's all it is, just being bad little girls—and boys—dirtying their pants." She was seething now. She swayed back and forth slowly. Her voice was raspy. "We should all sell out!"

"Sell out to dog-shooters and bank pirates! But there might be other systems, correspondences . . . ."

In spite of herself, she smiled at my rant. "Look, Granther. I appreciate your doctoring me at Tam's. Oh, think what you want, but don't give others the occasion for scandal. As for illness, God sendeth His rain."

"But death ain't rain!" I shouted.

I shoved the bag back in her arms and would not take it back, when she pressed it on me again.

She pleaded: "It's what congregations think that counts."

I spat it all out: "Like about Abram and you? Like about Henry and Moll?"

She pretended not to hear a word. She was a wall. "Churches count. You know that, Granther," she said.

"Then witches should group together too." I moved closer to her.

"They were damned for that before."

"Do you want witch-swimming to come back?" I asked.

She looked at the swaying trees. She had a thoughtless, wild animal determination in her now ugly, trembling mouth. I wanted to prick her all over with pins.

"You took your help where you could get it," I said.

"Never. You did that—and that cursed Tam. I've learned that our only hope comes from prayer. Witchcraft would have let me die." She would not look me in the face. She was lying and would not yield. "Women are debased by witchcraft, as Negroes by slavery," she preached with Henry's distracted air.

I said, "Witchcraft is the way the weak can combat the strong. It's changing the rules." The bitch!

Silent, she held firm but her shoulders trembled, and she almost dropped the parcel. I wanted to kiss her hard, to master her. She swayed like a lusty Catholic Madonna. I hurled at her: "Hold the Christ child up, Belle."

She laughed quickly; then seemed to consider what I said a sacrilege and grimaced in disgust. Out of frustration I grabbed her other hand, but she froze, then wrenched away, shoving the bundle against my stomach. All right, I took it now—a devils' bargain.

Then I followed her glance down the road into the gloaming. Someone was waiting farther down the road. Quickly Belle pretended not to notice. But I knew it was *Henry*! Like a bad actress, Belle spoke before her prompter. So now I had not only lost her confidence, but she was deceiving me as well. I was betrayed.

"It's dangerous to go your own way alone now, Granther," she said slowly, knowing I had seen Henry. She wanted me to see him! I was being lessoned. She added, "Think of Scot and Lizzy."

She had recanted. She could face even death now, but not disapproval—and I was thriving on disapproval.

I moved closer to her to spite Henry now. "But witches . . .."

She broke in: "A pact with the Devil always brings death. No more, Granther! Please, for God's sake!" I felt tiny as a doll. I wanted to bat her teeth out with my hammer. Her mouth pursed up in her new bulldog way. I mimicked it.

She smiled. "Sorry, Granther, I'm, I'm a bit daft right now." Then, as if revealing too much, she added, "A toothache I think."

"I'll be happy to pull it out."

She laughed. Then looked toward Henry. Without knowing it, I was holding her hand again, and dropped it. I could see Henry pacing angrily and probably praying in the smoky twilight. I was excited. Challenge Henry—yes! I asked, "Are you threatening me with black-balling?"

"No Christian would give up on another soul."

I wanted to give the pork and potatoes back, but why should her sacrifice obligate me? I was my own god now and could refuse or honor the suppliant. A bold insult was best: "I'll see you back home?"

"I'll do fine," she said. Looking down the road, she pulled her hand away. I said no more but stormed into the empty house. I was done playing the fool for her or anyone.

I tossed and tossed that night in bed, unable to arouse myself, even with Lizzy gone and Belle having been near. Intuition led me: I looked under the bed, and there was the leather cord with the nine knots of the ligature in it. A joke by Judy Rhines herself. I would have once been horrified and have stayed slack. But now I untied the knots that secured the spell of impotency, immediately was excited, and dropped to sleep.

CHAPTER 19

The next day being Sunday I did not go to the Boo but walked on my brittle legs to see Neil and Judy Rhines. The mist had disappeared, and the sun glared. The ligature! Neil had seen me meet Belle and was protecting me against lust—the Son of a Bitch! I brought the cord and put the ligature back in. Neil was shaving outside with his ax, a tin bowl of suds resting on a decayed wood pile. Judy Rhines was sitting, looking out of the window, expecting me. She wore a bright red housecoat, which made my clerical black and Neil's moleskin vest and leather trousers laughable.

I snapped the leather cord in the air, like a whip.

"Yes, I put it there, Granther," said Judy Rhines, taking the cord in through the window.

I spluttered, "Why in damnation?"

"I knew you would find it. I thought it would ease Liz's going. It was a joke."

Why was everyone suddenly meddling with me so? These devils and angels were fighting over my soul—but which was which?

"And it'll help your body too," Neil added, half his face lathered.

"Voodoo?"

"Well, sir," Neil said, waving his ax at me. "Thet ain't voodoo. Bet you felt better after untying those nine knots."

"Maybe I'll try the ligature on you, slave-boy," Judy said, reaching out and whipping Neil lightly on the back with the cord, as she handed me a jar of dire.

"Now Jude, don't be putting spells on me. I got troubles double."

I thought to reconcile them before Neil and Jude came at it. "The town has all-in-all against us," I said, sipping the dire.

Judy said, "The town hates the village. We are all trash now in their eyes. All whores. . . . .." She waved the cord in a circle above her head. Then the cord snaked itself into a slip knot, and she gibbeted her left wrist.

Neil jumped. "Jude!"

"It's true, let's say it, Granther. We're squeezed out of meeting. Even the Reverend Murray and the Universalists don't want us, for we're not 'spectable. Mollie and me are the local brothel for the Harbor people. The only answer we can make is witchcraft. Let's drown the mackerel fleet!"

Neil snapped, "Stop joking, Jude. Tam warned yer of yer jokin'."

Judy rolled her eyes at me. "Aunt Tam's content to visit, now. Thanks, Granther."

Neil said, "She knows this old shipwreck of a house'll go down soon, and we'll have to live with her. She's cursin' us all right."

Then like a musket charge, a white light exploded and flitted inside about the room, flying around Judy Rhines' head, a flying chunk of ice—or the winged skull of a child. "It's Jude's familiar," said Neil, "a wingy boy of snow." It shot up onto a rafter and froze to a lump of yellowy ice. I looked in and saw a hole in the roof. "It's hard to keep up wid everything in this village," Neil said, laughing. "Too much happening."

"Go in and get it Granther," Neil said. "We got it for you."

"'T's yourn, Granther. Take it with you," said Judy Rhines. "It was caught on one of Neil's rabbit traps. He tamed it for you."

I went inside, and Judy Rhines gave me a dead mouse.

I raised the mouse by the tail in my left hand and held my right arm crooked.

"No, Granther," Neil laughed. "Rub it with your hand. Make a light sushing."

As soon I did, the skull was there, snapped up the mouse, and landed on my shoulder. It gawked about, as if it were my protector. Judy Rhines tied the ligature around its leg. "Good luck, Granther," she said, "You'll need it. I looked into the tea leaves for you."

"It's the new American eagle," Neil said.

. . .

So I found Hoppo, an arctic owl driven down to Gloucester during that year of northern starvation, a few weeks of warm weather would have driven her back north, but the cold spring had kept her here for me—a sign, an omen, a prophecy. She drifted into my life like Start, another hobo from the north, and the reincarnation of that arctic owl that had died on the deck on our Atlantic crossing, a new totem.

I nailed a peach basket sideways to a tree trunk as a home for her. She began to filch chipmunks and shrews from Start and Abaijah and snatched the brown and white mice that gnawed about my house. The owl fast became a pet and was too quick for dogs to challenge. She stayed in the yard like a cat on a fence post and waited for the cats, who acted as her beaters, to drive out the shrews. With meat scraps, I taught her to come to the word "witch." Later I figured she could fend on her own, but at first I kept her in the yard, except when she followed me in the woods, staying a safe distance away from strangers and shadowing me home at a distance, like a ghost child.

Once during one of Henry's sermons against witchcraft, I heard Belle cry out, and I looked up. It was Hoppo, who at the word *witchery* had flown in the open door and circled just above the pulpit, beating her wings. Quickly I went to the back door to stir up trouble and waved my arms like an owl, which always drove her frantic. Others were now saying *witch,* meaning me, and Hoppo was following the word everywhere, trying to perch on their arms, which they flapped about like chicken's wings to keep her off and which made her claw them even more. My clumsy attempts to attract her looked like a mad attempt at a winged exit—"transvection," I called out. But my humor was backfiring.

When the congregation quieted, Hoppo flew to me. Some of the parishioners came out, and I thrashed about pretending that I was subject to conniptions, which made things worse. Now my own village might disown me out of shame, and word would no doubt reach Lizzie. Perhaps she would come back to save me.

I left Hoppo loose and heard reports of how she swooped down on unsuspecting gossips repeating the story with the key word, which gave her a legendary character. Many, seeing her only at night, said she was a flying death's head. Fearing she would be shot, I retethered her to a branch by a peach basket with the leather ligature cord. But she broke off the small branch on which the tether was tied and flew off with the branch in tow. Stories spread how a witch on a broom had been seen "flying across the moon's face." Another time, I told Reverend Davis in a moment of exasperation that Scot had come back in another form and pointed over his shoulder to Hoppo in her peach basket. My diabolic reputation in the Harbor Village grew.

All humor fell now under suspicion, especially mine; yet my jokes were a power over others, and it was mastery at all costs now. Others too, delighting in what was forbidden, sometimes caught the fever. Not to be cowed by anyone, Belle answered me back in kind by telling me that my other dead children were perched in the trees, like the unwashed children of Eve. Humor is a forerunner of madness. Many others dared grim pleasantries—when no one was around. Moll Jacobs asked me to put a cleft sole on her pumps, and Neil said that the price of witch poison has risen sharply in the Harbor Village. But if I tried to explain seriously to them the secret connections between words and things, they would write me off as a spouter. Worse, in public, they would only talk of keeping the earliest cucumber seeds for the following spring for they were the best—snore, snore.

Many took to spitting behind to avoid the effects of the evil eye. If I found huckleberries, someone said it was the result of the super-sensory powers I possessed. Once I cut a barrel in half and made two tubs, and that fool Sammy Maskey commended my "black art." Hoppo's chipmunks, shrews, and mice, ravished to pellets, were noted by Judy Rhines and Black Neil, who always claimed to know what I had in the "cauldron" that night.

But joking was soon to end.

CHAPTER 20

That Sunday the weather shot back to winter, though it was now April. But hunger drove me on. I got some horse bones from the well near Granny Day's swamp, and, towards sunset, I took my bait can, fishing poles, and bamboo rods wound with string and barbed pins and went to Fresh Pond on Eastern Point. I dug worms along the way, breaking the freezing ground with an ax. I had checked the glass: 28.5. I knew rough weather was in store. A blond carter boy from Lanesville, who drowsed all the time, gave me a ride. Before I reached the pond, there were snow squalls.

Neil had promised to be on hand. But when I arrived, I could not spot him. Since Fresh Pond is near the Harbor, many local fishers were there, relentlessly brushing rain and wet snow from their faces, hunting the water for food. I tossed in the horse bones to lure some fish.

Once in a while, a carp would jump in the air. I hoped it would catch a worm and get away; it deserved it for its work of cleaning the bottom. The water was getting too warm for trout from the dying, thick plants. It was not likely that carp or trout or pond would last much longer; besides an inlet from the sea was near to cutting through from Brace's Cove. But here in the New World, we had to make do. The waters of Europe were fished out, whatever losses we suffered here. There I was stuck again in trying to save something, unable to leave it, wallowing in my helplessness. The old humiliations, the old boulders I had to go back and remove. I was obsessed with unmovable boulders. I repictured Henry and Moll lying here upon her blue cloak. This time the memory delighted me. I should remind Belle of that soon and gain more advantage.

Standing nearer, I saw Roger and Red from the Gloucester Bank. I pulled my jockey cap down over my eyes. Quickly I set up my y-sticks and poles near where I had tossed the horse bones and soon began to jerk in the fish, while Red and Roger's lines stayed slack.

"What's your bait?" Red asked me, without so much as a hello, his hair freshly stiff with soap. He didn't recognize me.

"Little wormies," I said.

"Special worms?" He leaned closer.

"Dug them nearby, boys."

"So did we."

"It's luck," Roger said, the larger boy who was smoking his cigar of corn silk and chocolate.

"No, it ain't, boys," I said, whacking the trout on a rock.

"Well, what then?" the cigar said.

"It's craft."

"What you got we ain't got?" Roger added, while checking to see if it were the rain that had made his cigar go out.

"You have to make the fishes come to you," I said.

"Ah come on," said the cigar.

"Wait, Roger," Red said, in a snide way. "Listen. The magic man's gettin' the fish."

"Well," I said, pretending to be reading it out of the sky, "you have to be careful not to lean too far out over the water."

"Hell, we know that one, you old fool," said the cigar. "Shadows scare fish. But there ain't no shadows today."

"Did you know that cigars scare them too and red hair?"

"Go back below!" Roger said.

"Well, how come I got all the fish?"

"Yeah, how's that?" Red said to the cigar. "Witchery?"

"We caught 'em before you came," Roger said. "Yeh, you must be from Dogtown and a witch, aren't you? Well, you're a witch then. They're all witches up there."

Red smiled: "Them witches up there better look out, for them kucking stools can still be used. Right, Roger?"

Roger said, "Why don't they sell out up there. Let some fresh air in?"

Ignoring that, I said, "If I was a witch, I wouldn't bother with a fishing line. I'd just wait until you boys caught some fish"—my second pole began to drag towards the water, falling off its y-stick. I hurried after it. "Then, I would fill a tub with water and put some sticks in it and say, `Roger's fish. Red's fish.'" I pulled in a shimmering sixteen-inch trout.

"Hey, how did you know our names?" Roger asked. He had tiny, ugly brown teeth. He came closer, looking at me.

He knew me now, all right.

He said, "Red, let's toss witch man into the water."

Red looked about at the other fishers.

"Don't worry. They'll help us."

I ignored them. "Three times I would say that and your fish would come into my tub, and you would be eating hominy gruel again." Roger looked like he would throw his haymaker.

"Couldn't goddam' do better, myself." It was Judy Rhines, hidden in a purple kerchief. Behind her was Black Neil in gray oilskins.

"How do you do it?" Cigar said, pretending real interest, but afraid now. Red had already wound up his two sticks. Neil grabbed Roger's pole, broke it to a switch and was ready to lay into him, but Judy eyed him off.

"True, I wouldn't have known your names, if I weren't a witch. Your ma knows that," I said.

"Ma ain't no witch," Roger answered meekly.

"That's why you ain't got no fish," I said.

"Careful, Roger," Red said.

"Well then, you little boys better move on. I think you got a bite already," Judy said. One of Roger's poles was slipping fast into the water and went under before he could grab it.

"How did ya do that, Granther?" Neil asked. Roger heard behind him Neil whipping the air with half of Roger's pole, like a school birch, laughing with his great chompers gleaming in the sunless day.

Both boys stiffened.

"I'm the Black Man, the Devil hisself. You boys better behave."

Red and Roger tried to look collected. "You ain't no Devil," said Roger, backing off, "I seen you clerking the docks."

Then I turned and snapped my wrist in a quick cast. I whipped the cigar out of Roger's mouth. Then Neil cast Roger's broken pole, and the bent pin went through Red's ear. Red froze, blood trickling down his neck. Roger lit out without his poles and fish towards Plummer's Farm. Other fishers were watching closely now, as the blood ran hotter down from Red's ear. He stood as before a firing squad, as I unbent the barbed pin and eased it out and Jude smeared on her salve. I should have felt ridiculous working over these horrid urchins, but I didn't, though I wanted bigger game now and knew it would come.

"Initiation's over," Judy laughed. "Go home, little boy." Red rattled off like shot.

"This'll lead to more scandal," I said, starting to falter.

"Tut," Judy Rhines said. "This is more fun than stopping wagons or piling pumpkins."

She laughed. "Now they'll believe you a real witch."

"They can go to Armageddon, the fuckin' brats," I said.

Judy said, "Granther, you smell like a witch."

"Lard and sweat, I think," Neil said.

"No, witches have a certain smell," Judy Rhines boomed out.

"What about me?" Neil asked, picking up the trout the boys left. "Do I have the odor of sanctity?"

"I've never smelled that," said Judy Rhines, "You just stink slave, but Granther he stinks witch."

Neil laughed, and the soles of my feet tingled with cold. Let what had to come, come.

. . .

When I returned home, I found Lizzy tending the cooking fire. We said nothing to each other after our months of separation. Scot was nowhere in sight.

CHAPTER 21

A few nights later, she tossed and tossed in bed, talking nonsense in her sleep. In the morning, when she tried to get out of bed, she fell to the floor.

That April remained the coldest and wettest ever. Lizzy lay ill for days, often unconscious. Doctors seldom came to Dogtown, since they seldom got their fees, and the village reputation for the unsanitary had become proverbial. In those moments when she could talk, she said that in Haverhill she had visited a doctor who was ill himself but too greedy to interrupt his practice. He had examined her twice and had dismissed her illness as the green-apple two step. He told her to change her diet of cabbage soup and wouldn't listen to how long she had been ill. She believed him, however, and, a few days later she thought she had recovered and started for home. Scot too wanted to return, but she told him to remain at Granny Goody's farm in Haverhill till she sent for him.

Lizzy became pale as summer sky and hotter. She said her heart-beat was enough for two and her head throbbed. Some days she would eat nothing and stalked about in a housecoat, shrinking inside it, like the cats who, locked by chance in the Boo, starved to death. The journey must have weakened her. Maybe she had come back to die with me.

Outside, the village fell into the last stages of decay and had reverted to its original wilderness. Most of the families moved to Gloucester, while a few, like us, walled themselves up in the immobility of their cabins, as if to shrink and disappear. Mostly widows with dogs were left, and, as these women died, more dogs would join our pack whose barking now brought a sound like the crashing of the tide to the heights of Dogtown. I often woke raving myself and at times wanted to slit Lizzy's throat and mine to save us the pain.

I went to the Harbor to find work but was scorned and abused. As soon as Lizzy was an inch better, we would take the stage to Haverhill.

But Lizzy turned worse, her body pale and cold as cheese. Belle and Henry came to help me. Belle improvised prayers. Henry tried traditional ones, verses from the Old-Testament prophets, while I resorted to magic, black as well as white. Two doctors, called by Henry, came and hurriedly went, leaving pills that changed nothing.

One Sunday morning I left Lizzy to the care of Judy Rhines and Black Neil and went to Henry's to pray. Belle stood out in the bright sunlight, a green dress beside our buckrams. The three of us were ready to go to meeting.

I prayed:

> Manitou, Great Spirit who inspired the powwow,
> Who brought the tall stones from the north,
> Lord of All Souls, red and white and black,
> Great Fox who hunts the Salmon River

The Same that fed Elijah among the Syrian rocks,
Punish us not—beyond our endurance.
Help us withstand your judgments.

I believed in the spirits of the New World to cure New-World dis-
eases, but I stood helpless to form a traditional prayer, not that
Scripture was unknown to me. I had studied well at Harvard College
and recalled even my "damned" Latin, as I read the *Hammer of
Witches,* but I tossed between fear and anger—fear that I had delved
into magic at all and had brought on Lizzy's illness and anger that no
God—just life itself—was trying us too much on the headland of Cape
Ann. Belle's indictment was just: something—history or geography or
Harbor society—had leased us all to perdition. Perhaps there was no
one to blame—that was worst of all. Thinking such things, I couldn't
pray in the usual sense. What was there to pray to? Henry and Belle
looked at me mournfully, as if I were a chicken trampled by an ox. I
dared not think of Belle now.

Unable to go to meeting, I wandered back to the sickbed distracted. The sky had swaddled itself in cloud. When I arrived I saw outside,
on either side of the doorway, our two tipped-over rusty blueberry pails
that Lizzy and I had used since we were married. We wouldn't use them
again.

But the door was open, and the oil paper on the windows was
tacked tight—and the smell of cornbread wafted from the open door! I
could have leapt the Commons Bars for joy! Prayers must have moved
rocks. But it was Judy Rhines who poked her head from the open doorway. Lizzy was propped in a chair at the table, looking at the heat
steaming out into the cold. She seemed a corpse already, wrapped in
white blankets, stained yellow, a pillow her halo. She raised her finger
and smiled idiotically to assure me—if she knew it was me!—that all
was well, like some lame-brained bishop, giving a blessing. I hated and
feared her at that moment. Perhaps I would even be blamed for her
sickness and death.

While I stood there in a stupor, Judy and Black Neil began furiously hurling clothes out of the house.

Neil said, "Gotta eat, Liz. Cornbread fleshes ya' bones, nor no mo' huskings for yer."

Lizzy smirked and pecked at a bit of cornbread like a pigeon. Her nose, now more defined by her thinness, gave her face the gauntness of death. I went cold: life itself was killing her. But at least she could eat.

Judy Rhines nodded me outside.

Judy said, "Granther, it's typhus fever. She must have caught it from the Haverhill people. There's an epidemic there, now."

The doctor! Now we would have to stay. And nothing to be done! In a rage, I ran at Lizzy, trying to smash down the stone wall that always stood between us: "No, no!" and buried my head between her knees. Lizzy laughed the little that she was able. In my fury, I pulled up her nightdress. Close up I could see the red pimples and bluish spots on her stomach. She tried to push me back, giggling her embarrassment. I pushed closer, kissing her bare stomach, trying, trying to get the disease myself. Neil pulled me off. My stomach froze and the soles of my feet. Lizzy kept fidgeting with the blankets, her white skeletal fingers snapping at the edges like starving gulls. Then she held her head that must have pained her greatly, and I backed away.

"Are we going to die in this fucking place?" I screamed.

"Never mind, Granther," said Neil, slapping me softly on the ear. "I seen it in Orleans. We need to kill the lice. Clean hard!"

Sobered, I got up, and Neil and I started throwing clothing and bed clothes outside. Judy had brought clean ones. I became conscious and tried to shoo them home, "The infection!"

"Granther," joked Judy, "I'm a witch, so is Neil."

I appealed to Lizzy to no avail. I could tell from her gawking that she wanted to see, so I dragged her outside in the chair.

It looked like an abandoned gypsy camp, the clothes scattered about the yard, our life in rags. We piled the clothes together with hoes and rakes, then soaked them in whale oil, and lit them.

It began to drizzle.

The dampness from the rain made the smoke suffocating. It billowed a balloon of yellow fog and, in a sudden swirl of wind, bit our eyes. Lizzy coughed and was losing breath, so Judy and I carried her to the Boo in her chair, as if it were a stretcher, and Neil stayed to tend the fire.

When I returned, Neil had straightened the fire so that the smoke funneled in a narrower stream. I could see the flames twisting into a hook-nosed crone that was Lizzy, bent by disease. I recalled the survivors of the plague burning their dead in bone-fires. Then she changed to Belle, in a white-silk gown, consumed even faster by the yellow fire roiling up in a twister of gray smoke.

When the wind lurched again against me, but before the smoke stung my eyes shut, I caught flashes from Neil's horse teeth. Wielding his hoe like some demon, Neil looked the Black Man himself, making a Bonfire of the Vanities of the New World.

"We burn these heretic lice, Granther, don't fret none," he called gently and brought me back to the Commons.

"Has Thomazine got Jude back now, Neil?" I asked, rubbing my eyes, trying to think of anything else but Lizzy.

"Hell, Granther, Jude feels all those pains and aches that Tam sends her so bad she can't sleep at night. And you know what Judy says? She says Tam got fat to hide her big tits from men. How you gonna put those two cats in the same bag?" Neil spun his hoe in the air, like a trick military drill, and caught it.

"Is Thomazine a witch?"

"Tam's a witch, the most important witch in the Commons, which is something these days. Know what I think?" Part of Neil's moleskin vest caught sparks. He crushed them against his side with his bare upper arm. "Someone needs to steal that witch power and use it for all us. And for Lizzy. For Lizzy, yessir. You, Granther!—you were educated and yer ma was a healer." I rubbed my stinging eyes the more. Neil went on, "Someone's gotta cure Lizzy." He stuck his hoe in the ground at parade rest.

"How's that?" I asked, squinting through the smoke to spot Lizzy.

Neil shouted at me: "I see Marie Laveau run the mayor of Orleans. I did." Neil passed the hoe to me, and I began raking our few unburnt clothes, like dead souls, into the fire.

A corner of the land caught on fire, driving the insects into exodus: spiders, ants, chafers, may beetles, bulbous insects unknown to me, all escorted by air-bourne skippers, trooped across the road, smoked out. It was a grand retreat, like a Russian village fleeing Bony's army. All these had hid in the fields grazed over by oxen and cows, all unseen, more than I could have dreamed up for the Noah's ark I made for Scot.

We put the field fire out with feet and blankets. Except for what we were wearing, our clothing had burned away. Our souls, Lizzy's and mine and Scot's, were free now, free of their old selves. I peered into the cotton batting of the sky, into the bandage of smoke over the sun's eye. A sense of freedom and fight chilled me, as if I were a crab molting, shedding my old warm shell from tender skin—the liberation of the acceptance of death. The cold backed off, and I felt the heat of the sun's eye through the clouds.

The burning had taught me that, if the power of nature is attacking, bounce back its power, brace like the ram against its charger, the cliff against the wind, the oppressor's rock against the *oppressor's* chest. The Principle of Return. I recalled simple verses from the Black Book. But it was six o'clock in the afternoon, not the hour of Jupiter, under whose dominion, healing is best performed, but that of Mars Netos, under the angel Zamael, the hour of overthrowing enemies, still I mumbled:

> O Salamanders of the Fire, I call you,
> By Him who shall burn the world clean one day,
> Burn and torment my enemies.

Be a wall of protection to me
By Aleph, Mem, Shin.

It tasted in my mouth like such a sour stew of words I laughed as the wind wrenched the smoke and fire south toward the Harbor. I now *knew* it was what you convinced yourself of that worked and one faith was as good as another. This old witchery that perhaps went back to ancient rites gave me the solace and the illusion of power and hope, while Cape Ann Christianity was wearing out in sectarian squabbles. As I eyed Neil, absorbed in raking the fire's last remnants, pretending not to hear my invocations, I saw a human shape again in the last of the smoke. It was Belle, coming for me. Neil almost shattered the image with his rake, but it embraced me, till, at a crack that seemed loud enough to make another Whale's Jaw of some rock, thunder opened the trap of heaven and the rain poured out abundantly. I walked back to the Boo in prayer.

At the threshold, Judy said, "She's taken another turn for the worse." Lizzy was unconscious, barely breathing, the way a baby sleeps. We carried her back home from the Boo in one of the blankets Judy Rhines had brought, and I wrapped her in some of Judy's ticking.

I turned to my book of magic. That was all I had now. I read every incantation against ague, as I waited till the favorable hour. I read that the French of the last century lay on the tomb of Deacon Paris, the Jansenist, and cures, attributed to the Devil by the Catholic Church, were brought about by the Deacon who had conspired with the Fiend. He had cured a Demoiselle Coirin of shriveled leg and a breast cancer so quickly that she healed overnight and was sitting before her dresser the next morning, where her lady-in-waiting found her at her toilet. I accepted the doubtful hearsay of literature.

As if my devilish prayers were answered, Sammy Maskey appeared at the Boo that night.

He had a white cloth in his hand. He said nothing but opened it in the candlelight, and I saw some blue rot from some decayed vegetable.

I wanted again to hammer the silliness out of him, but it was too late. "Humor, Granther. Keep your heavenly humor. What's witchcraft, Granthers, without it? And this is witchcraft, let's say it and get it over with. Go, take this mold to Lizzy. Tell her it is cheese and feed her some. It is the right day, being the tenth day after the fever started, and I have cast the times and the planets are with us."

I followed Sammy's solution repulsive as it was.

. . .

The next morning I woke up, and Lizzy was sitting up in bed, fixing her hair.

"Recovered! Miracles! You're recovered! Sitting up, doing your hair!"

"Better, now," Lizzy chirped, though her color was only less pale than the stained blankets.

Afraid to approach her—fearing it was her astral self—I finally wrestled down my fears and grabbed her too hard in my arms. But she only laughed: "Easy, Granther."

"Lizzy!" I sang it, "Lizzy!"

Lizzy said, "Still weak, Morgan, but better."

Reddening at the ensuing silence, she said, "I saw that silly snoop Mistress Maskey, peering in the window a while ago."

"Did he see you?" I asked, hoping Lizzy would not get curious.

"Yes, I think so. Do you do business with that little thief, too?" She bunched her hair up a bonnet and put her hands on her ears and swung her head side to side the way Sammy did.

I laughed, overjoyed. I was about to say that Sammy Maskey and witchery cured her, when Lizzy squeaked, eyeing me, "But I wouldn't make a pact with the Devil for a recovery like this."

I answered her, "Don't rave like that, Lizzy. You don't know what you're blathering about. Ha, ha. Your fever must be still hot."

. . .

All that next night, the first I had slept in almost ten days, I heard Judy's whinnying laughter till it changed into village cheers for Sammy Maskey as the great "Witch of Dogtown." Then a dream headache came, most severe, as after a husking-bee. Then I dreamed I had woken to find my masculinity gone. My skin was smooth and hairless to the thighs. Fear froze me. I feigned illness with Lizzy and dreaded that she would see my loss while I slept.

In my dream, I went to Sammy Maskey's house in my nightshirt in full daylight. There was my witch hex on his door, but Sammy didn't answer. I ran to the meetinghouse, but it was a ruin: broken windows; the glass and feathers and bird white strewn all through the inside. I heard rats in the loft. I looked out the window frame: the village was all abandoned.

I found myself at Thomazine's. Her house was the only one intact. There was the pyramid of pumpkins, but fresher than before. The little window swung open. Thomazine appeared now a young and seductive witch, her gray hair, now black, standing out in astral points around her bare head.

"Lost youself, Granthers?" The voice was not hers but Sammy Maskey's. She, or he, continued, "A bird took it to an oak tree on Lamb's Ledge. It nests there in the third V of the oak."

Barefoot, I limped up Lamb's Ledge, my knees more glass than ever. The sun beat down on my hatless head. Only one old oak was visible and sure enough there was a nest in the third V. There was no difficulty in reaching the first V. The second was a sweaty climb. From there I could reach, but not see into, the third nest. I reached up and quickly drew my hand away. It felt like a pit full of slugs. I shinnied up to the nest, my glass legs being given new life. I looked in the nest, and there were many members twisting about eating barleycorns.

I reached for the biggest one. Sammy's voice came from Thomazine's youthful head below. "That's Reverend Davis'. Yours is the second biggest." Shame and laughter overcame me at once. In anger, Thomazine shook the tree. I fell down into her arms. But it was Lizzy.

She was still very weak, and I barely heard her. "You're raving, Granther. Come to!"

I woke and clutched myself. I was as hard as an oak branch.

"What have I been saying?"

"Just nonsense, Granther."

"It's typhus fever. I feel it on my tongue." I stuck out my tongue.

"There's not a spot on you, Granther. It is all inside your skull. Your head is as cool as Peter's Pulpit."

True, I didn't have the disease. But what had I said in my sleep? What did I owe now for Lizzy's recovery? Was the Devil, or whatever it was, going to get me before the town kucking gangs would, after hearing more of my witchery? Would Lizzy someday know that witchery saved her? My guilty mind was corroding.

CHAPTER 22

It was now safe to call Scot back from Haverhill.

About a week after his arrival with clothes for us, I arrived home from the Boo after putting lifts on Lizzy's boots and carrying them home. I had finished off some dire and was a bit at sea on my feet. The sun-red rays lit up a witch hex nailed to my door: four sticks woven in the shape of an hour glass, with a fifth stick flexed vertically through to bind them in place. Through the slightly open shutter, I could make out Lizzy with a fork poking a chicken blackening on the fire spit. Where did she get the fowl? I kicked the door open, stepped to the puncheon table, sat, and slammed the hex on the table beside me for her to see. Scot must have made it.

Without looking at me, Lizzy said, "Granther, you must stop, stop this superstitious witch play. Witchcraft will kill us all." She began to whimper. I can't stand whimpering.

I said, "I saved you. Should I have let you go down?"

"Witches go to hell!"

"Scot!" Lizzy said.

He was moving towards me from the corner where I couldn't see him. Well, sure. They had been talking me up.

"You're making a damn fool of yourself, father," Scot said. Had he been drinking?

"What the hell have you been telling him, woman?" I asked.

"No more than Henry says about how you go about with witches. Scot went to the harbor for work, but your cursed reputation followed him!"

We looked at one another. So Henry had brought the chicken. "What the hell do you know about witchery, Lizzy? Though if you had had your way after the others died, you would have had witches' brew instead of Scot."

I had not meant to say that, ever, but murder will out. Lizzy paled. Scot lurched towards me, but his mother's tears checked him, and he held off, wavering. A fortunate split in the forces against me.

"You didn't want him. Remember? All the pain you said, lying about how you were sick all the carrying time, wishing you were dead, and it was all in your brain because of the others. Then you wanted a potion, but I refused to get it. You wanted witchery, then. And there was Abram Wharf."

It was as if the Devil spoke, instead of me, a Devil who had been waiting in me, while I worked on Lizzy's cure. Now the Devil walked in my body and spoke out, against my will. Lizzy winced as I moved closer to her, curling my fist. The floorboard creaked beneath my boot. Lizzy stared at the floor without seeing it, her bottom lip covering her upper. Something powerful drove me against them, the more I wanted to help them. I stepped closer.

Scot jumped between us: "No, father!" Now I smelled the dire on his breath. I couldn't lose the mastery in my own house. I grabbed Scot by the shoulders to fling him aside, but he butted me with his chest and I stumbled backwards, dizzy with dire, against the chicken and the fire. A wave of sparks exploded up the wall. Crouching against the wall for support, I sprang back, shaking off the beads of flame starting to singe my back. I could still do Scot, and Scot sensed it, even though we were the same height and my son heavier. Scot wavered and didn't attack.

"You fucking monkey," I roared, "Who put you up to this?"

Lizzy was sucking her upper lip, and Scot went voiceless and looked at her. I saw the witch hex that Scot had nailed to the door lying on the table. With one hand, I pulled his jaw around. "Look," I said, "Wear this. You'll need it." I broke it across Scot's face and stood there holding a piece of it to Scot's eye. Then Scot lashed at me with his fists, striking me on either ear. I punched his cheek and knocked him down. Then sat on his chest, slapping his head side to side, a hex piece still in my hand and scratching his face. Scot was now crying, his mouth streaming blood.

"I am trying to save your lives," I said.

"Get away from him," Lizzy yelled and shoved a flaming stick from the fire into my face. I swung and hooked her hip and knocked her back. She shouldered the door open and fell over the threshold stone, the brand flying into the night.

"Stay away," Scot cried, slapping the hex piece from my hand. Then that Devil relented. I looked down at Scot. Remorse set in. I wanted to be sorry for what was happening to us, to the Commons Settlement. Instead, I sprang a leak. "Don't you care anything about your father? The whole town is ganging up on him, like he is some stray dog, and you let it happen. You with your fine Spanish leather boots. Prancing is all you care for and for your ma who didn't want you."

Scot looked up, bewildered. I saw the strong pact too strong against me. I got off Scot and pulled Lizzy up who was crying too. Then Scot jumped up but shrunk back, hesitating. Lizzy picked up the chicken with a fork and shoved it in the fire bucket. The steam burst around her face, like a medium at a seance. I grabbed the chicken from her, singing my hands, and spitted it with the piece of the hex, and walked away. I saw the brand Lizzy had come at me with still burning in the dark in front of the house.

As I staggered back toward the Boo, I felt followed. Out of the crack of my eye, I could see Scot, circling me like Judy's Elva. But he didn't attack, just watched until he was sure that I was inside and had not taken the path to the tavern. Then he went back to the house.

I fed pieces of chicken to Hoppo, not eating any myself.

"In fact, she's dead."

At the words, I spun around.

It was Thomazine, standing before me, proclaiming, like the Angel of Death himself. Her face buried in her black wishbone and her body wrapped in her rotten sumac-colored shawl.

Trembling, I asked, "Who's dead, Tam?"

"Belle," she said softly. "Belle."

She whispered, "It's the death of the Commons."

Then she vanished as quickly as she had come.

I had turned into a Dogtown rock.

"I must visit Henry," I finally said to the air. And all the ruin and guilt of the world poured in on me. I was cold as ocean water. I had been afraid only for myself, attacking Scot and Lizzy because *I* was afraid, fighting ghosts. Why be afraid? I felt black shame, now thinking of my paltry life—the death of the woman I dreamt about! I had been living on false hopes—till now.

CHAPTER 23

Must go to the village! Belle's funeral. "In fact, she's dead." In fact.

Three days later Belle`s funeral was to be performed by the Reverend Hammett much to the dismay of Henry who wished to perform it himself. He was, however, too thunderstruck. He had made the rounds of the houses in the village begging folk to pray for themselves as well as for his dead wife. But his voice rang hollow as the wind whistling off the boulders, not in the old hollow way, when he drifted to some secret place while he preached, but now strengthless, like the dead. Even Henry didn't believe anymore.

She was to be buried in the West Parish Burying Ground, unlike the majority of us in Paupers' Fields or the roadway—and with a name. The service was to be in the new First Parish Church they said, because she was a minister's wife and well known, but really because Reverend Hammett still wished to close our meeting-house on the Riverdale Green. Many would turn out, not for Belle, but to see what us Commons villagers had degenerated into, a side show of witches for the many new migrants to Gloucester: Swedes, Portuguese, Canadians, French, and Irish. Along with the Harbor people, they all learned to scant what was now called "Dogtown"—and the "dogs." Many of our dogs had been killed, preying upon the town. Hoppo too had either flown off or been killed by some farmer.

In our high anger and rags and the dire we had sipped, we walked along Cornhill toward First Parish Church, a sorry cortege on foot, as no one would give us a ride now. But we were noticed by all: me in my shabby buckram, Judy Rhines a cloak French blue ("and her going to a funeral!"), Neil in a gray frock coat, borrowed from Henry, thrown over his leather breeches and moleskin vest, and Lizzy looking like a respectable keeper of the insane in her black taffeta and black cloak, once worn by her Presbyterian mother.

Cowed by the city that was destroying us, we gawked at sights that kept our minds, for a moment, off death. Our wood, which we had once cleared, formed the new houses along the new waterfront. The familiar octagonal windmill that dominated the harbor and once showed its old world origins was a reminder that we belonged no more in this new world of international trade—nor to the old world, for the mill not only no longer powdered wheat, but was up for sale, busted vanes and all. It was Tappan's Hotel that beckoned now, and only to wealthy investors. Beyond were the whitewashed ramparts of Fort Point Hill, forbidding in their spruceness. Since in recent years our visits to the town were infrequent, we had lost touch with the world growing around us. Now at leisure and to avoid remembering happier days, we craned at the skyline, as we paced about the city, waiting for the funeral to begin. The world was reaching for the sky in 1830. Spires and masts shot up like spears raised in some battle against poverty that we were losing in Dogtown Commons. Baptist, Universalist,

Congregationalist, all raised their tower lances against each other, though in union with ship chandlers and bank pirates. Thomazine said Belle's death was the death of the Commons, as it had been of my loving dreams. What *had* I meant to Belle?

"Samuel Gilbert, Outfitters," Neil remarked at the corner of Front and Commercial. The wagon I had sold fish from was at rest in front, as if it had waited for me all this time.

Judy rapped on the window.

"It's Old Nick," she shouted and laughed.

"It's the Old Terror himself," Neil Finson said, banging on the window.

"Maybe they don't like niggers," Judy Rhines said.

Neil laughed. "They forgot to know what one was, till Dogtown foundered on its rocks."

Like a clocktower mannikin, Mr. Squirrel Gilbert popped out the door. He threw a gray bundle, tied with a rope, into the street, opening and closing the door quickly, ignoring our presence. Plainly, he had recognized us.

"Oilskins," I said. "They dump the used ones out—like us—when they get so ragged no one would buy them again any more." Neil picked up the bundle, untied the rope, and smelled it and turned up his nose; then opened the door and hurled the bundle back in. Nothing was heard inside. Through the window we saw Mr. Gilbert berating a shop-boy about the oils. It was the blond Lanesville boy who had driven me to Fresh Pond to fish. But the boy was afraid to challenge us by throwing the skins out again. Proprietor Gilbert then sailed about the shop examining objects to give a show of busy-ness. From time to time, he looked up to see if we were gone, or to spy the constable. We kept our noses pressed against the window, rapping loudly.

Neil laughed, opened the door, and stepped in, followed by Judy Rhines and me.

"Good morning, Mr. Halliday," Gilbert said coldly.

Now he nodded to the Lanesville boy who ran by us headlong for the constable.

I said, "'Seems all the help's not native."

"Respectable community, Lanesville," Mr. Gilbert chirped.

"Ram fuck, we're not 'spectable!" said Neil, moving further into the shop. Judy howled her horse laugh. My shoulders shook with cold, feeling Lizzy's eyes upon my back.

"Shush," said Judy Rhines. "Remember poor Belle." Again she boomed her laughter.

Outside, Lizzy looked in, outraged, her hands shook beyond control. I pitied her. She looked like she would bolt or faint—she hardly had much strength left after the walk from Dogtown.

"Bacchus and his rout are coming," Judy said to Gilbert. Neil yowled at this. Bacchus had been an ex-slave who had scared the white children of Gloucester because Negroes were scarce there after the War for Independence. He still remained in bogey-man stories.

"He won't be here long," Gilbert said, with bravado, checking his spectacles by holding them up to the skylight.

He added, "If you are looking for Mistress Davis' funeral, you'll have to go back to your Meetinghouse Green, for she's being buried from Fourth Parish, after all. Reverend Hammett has closed First Parish Church because of the conflict with the Unitarian members."

His smirk told me he wasn't lying.

We looked at each other. We had been duped into not attending the funeral.

Lizzy nodded that the constable was coming.

. . .

Witchery gave us speed, for before we knew it, we stood before Fourth Parish Meetinghouse. Even Lizzy was invigorated now by anger.

But the rapid deterioration of our meetinghouse was a scandal. I had not seen the building for so long. Money had been kept from us by Hammett who wanted the meetinghouse taken down to increase his own parish. Always so well-kept, it now looked like a factory with an incongruous fire-bell tower attached to it, as if there had been a decorous church on the other side that was now missing. If I had been ordained, I would have been given just such a barn to prop up. The once elegant tower was square and made of brick, capped by the graciously lithe columns of its delicate lantern. Farther up, a dome lifted; then it shot its greenish copper-covered spire into the sky, gutting a rusted wind cock.

Inside, beside the pulpit on the north side were two long benches with high backs like settles. In one, Henry was slumped. Neil turned away and went to sit in the eastern part of the church that everyone knew was once reserved for Negroes. Judy laughed at his obstinacy, but he ignored her and stayed, insensitive even to Henry's grief and would not look at him. We found Moll Jacobs, sitting in a front pew. She wore a burgundy cloak like Belle used to—it *was* Belle's cloak! Henry must have given it to her for the funeral. Judy Rhines pushed me in first so I would be between Moll and her in a pew in the front center, away from Lizzy. Given the occasion and our reputation, the pew's owner would never confront us. Lizzy waited, standing at the back of the meetinghouse.

Then, when several boys, including Red and Roger, started whispering "witch" and "kucking stool" at her, she turned white and came down and sat with us.

Reverend Hammett was just coming in, unlike other ministers who were there early to greet their flock.

"Late," Lizzy said.

"With good reason," Moll said, "Last week he was fined twenty dollars for starving his pigs. He's shamefaced."

"The bastard should resign," Judy Rhines said, "Wasn't he fined last year for drunkenness? And *didn't* he carry on with Belle?" She watched me carefully as she said this. I winced under the blow. So we were witnessing Henry's humiliation—and Neil knew it. Lizzy bowed her head and prayed.

The wind picked up, and the old building creaked its timbers like the ride to America, though it should have been the ride to Heaven. Many parishioners had stopped coming because of the sordid condition of the old building. Today the wind sprites were worse than ever, as if they knew they would soon have to leave.

The service bell tolled. The Reverend Hammett, hardly looking at the congregation, walked to meet the casket, now set before the altar by unknown pall bearers—Henry had not been consulted. All stood up with the muffled clatter of bereaved congregations. When I first glanced at the casket, I thought how many I had made. Yet it drew me on and gave me comfort, as rites always do, the finely polished black box reflecting on its surface and in its silver nameplate and in its silver clasps the sparkling points of candlelight like stars, until it was a ship of lights leading out of this world. It was Belle somehow still dragging me on, forcing a kind of humor on all of us, a jolly Harvest Home, leading us from Dogtown. My head spun, thinking of her great, tainted spirit. For the first time now, I had to think of her as indeed gone and that my own death was near. Let them take me too.

"I think the reverend's been drinking this morning," Lizzy whispered, giving me a sermonette.

Reverend Hammett walked in front of the casket and intoned. *"I am the resurrection and the life, saith the Lord; he that believeth in me, though he were dead, yet shall he live; and whosoever liveth and believeth in me, shall never die."*

"There's hope for me, Granther," said Moll Jacobs, "Never say die."

Lizzy shot a glance at me across Judy, asking me to concur in Moll's damnation.

"*Witch, witch,*" the boys murmured up through the rafters, and I half-hoped that Hoppo would fly back in. But he had been lost like so many other things that I scarcely noticed till now. No matter.

"What about businesses?" Moll whispered. "Are they resurrected too? Mine's flat broke." She giggled drunkenly. "Little sailor money."

Henry stared at the candles rather than the casket sparkling with lights and then turned his head toward me and smiled, so he knew all along about Belle too. She had probably told him everything. How could people live that way? Now he was forgiving me, the condescending hypocrite! Belle was linking us together, welding us of the Commons into one family, even Reverend Hammett, was linking us in death and sin.

"We brought nothing into this world, and it is certain we shall carry nothing out."

"There you are now," Lizzy said to Moll, "All this worrying about things and life." She was a tough nut to crack.

"The Lord gave, and the Lord hath taken away."

I heard Molly mumble, "They could pay more often and beat you less, those fuckin' chums. Neil should protect me."

"Lord, let me know mine end, and the number of my days; that I may be certified how long I have to live."

Judy whispered, "Only sorcery can tell that, right, Granther?"

". . . and verily every man living is altogether vanity."

"Amen," Lizzy said, too loudly.

"Witch. Witch," echoed everywhere.

Hammett did not hear or ignored. His moon-face and fluttering hands moved about: *"For man walketh in a vain shadow, and disquieteth himself in vain; he heapeth up riches, and cannot tell who shall gather them."*

"Poor Neil," Judy Rhines sighed.

Reverend Hammett raised and spread his deathly hands in air.

"Deliver me from all mine offenses; and make me not a rebuke to the foolish."

Lizzy eyed me, but I sank into the angry, dark cave of myself.

"When thou with rebukes dost chasten man for sin, thou makest his beauty to consume away, like as it were a moth fretting a garment."

Lizzy glanced at my whitening hair, and I stared at her sunken cheeks. She was so gaunt she looked toothless. Her chin curved toward her nose. *Save her, save her!*

The Man in the Moon said, *"God is our hope and strength, a very present help in trouble."*

"This is the part about witches' power," Moll said, bobbing her head irreverently.

"Therefore will we not fear, though the earth be moved, and though the hills be carried into the midst of the sea; Though the waters thereof rage and swell, and though the mountains shake at the tempest of the same." Reverend Hammett's face was bed-sheet white.

Moll said, "They love witchcraft, these Harbor people. Watch." Moll drew Reverend Hammett's eyes with hers down her body to her fork. Standing in front of them, he tried not to look, but had no choice. She looked like Belle.

Reverend Hammett turned toward the casket. Moll stared hard at the minister. She caught his eye. I could see her glamour on him, so I moved about a bit jumpy to cast a spell too. A glamour might daze him. So I grappled my eyes onto Hammett's. I could feel Hammett shamed at being caught distracted by Moll's come-on and feared my condemning eye. It was the moment for my power. Like the basilisk, I drove my eyes, like Thomazine's green lamps, into Hammett, who couldn't pull his glance away.

The preacher intoned, *"I will lift up my thighs—eyes—unto the hills."*

"Witch. Witch." Louder reverberations.

Hammett reddened, and I eased off. He regained control by holding onto the altar rail, like a life boat. *"The Lord shall preserve thee from all evil."* I caught his eyes on Moll again. She turned her glance to the floor in mock modesty, corkscrewed her hair, as Belle did, and I caught him up again.

"Yea, it is even he that shall keep thy foul—no- thy soul!"

"Told you he was drunk," Lizzy said, giddy herself.

"Witch!" Louder still now from the rowdies. *"Kucking Stool!"*

"O let thine ears consider well the voice of my complaint."

I looked at Moll: benevolence shone in her face, like the Catholic Virgin—a sunbeam was making her radiant and young once more! Her younger self was burning through. Transfiguration! Henry saw it too. She was Belle sanctified! Hammett still fixed his eyes on Moll, as he must have on Belle when they started their affair, and he shook his head with mortification and jealousy and fear, as if this were a judgment on him. He gripped the rail, as if he were drowning, trying to keep his birdlike hands from shaking. His moon face loomed above us. I threw another glamour hard. Our eyes met. The wind sang in the dark rafters.

"*Witch!*"

Henry was in a dream. Moll raised her head and tried to smile at him. Judy winked to Neil who caught on. Lizzy was off praying hard to herself, eyes shut. We were inflicting revenge on the harbor. We wanted Henry to see. But he was weeping.

The minister mounted the pulpit. We sat down.

"The lesson for today is taken from the Old Testament. It is from *I Samuel 28.13: I saw gods ascending out of the earth.*" Henry stared open-mouthed, like a chorister, at the speaker.

That was a witch text. Hammett was stirring up trouble now, and everyone felt it. Judy Rhines looked at me to share her hatred. I did. We braced ourselves. What came was worse than we expected in our progressive century.

Hammett gained force, as if he had been saving his hate: "These are the words that the Witch of Endor says to Saul, which she freely confesses, because Saul has told her not to be afraid of his earlier admonitions against conjuring the dead, because he has given her royal leave."

"Hear ye, hear ye," Moll whispered.

"But the punishment for unlawful witchery in the Old Testament is death, and Our Lord does not remand that injunction in the New. Hence we must believe that only through some divine permission the dead can come back through witchcraft, but only through the power of the Lord and for a specific purpose: here to teach Saul the bitter wisdom that he shall lose the Kingdom of Israel. There *is* witchcraft then—good and *evil* witchcraft."

"*Witch-craft.*" echoed from the young men, as an antiphon.

Hammett pretended not to hear and tried hard to focus his sottish eyes on us. I frowned, how could Belle . . .?

But Henry showed no anger. He was watching Moll, now haloed by the aureole of window light that played up the golden highlights in her fiery hair: Moll *was* the reincarnation of Belle. We all looked: me, Hammett, Judy Rhines, Neil—even Lizzy. Belle was linking us further. The casket lights burnished brighter and melded together almost to unbearable sunlight.

In fact, she lives.

I stared at Moll. She was the World, the Mystery Itself, the Other. She was leading us out—transformed, recreated into other Creation, into Death and beyond Death. We were all right now.

Hammett now would not glance away from her: "Yes, the Church freely admits that witchcraft can perform miracles, but those miracles are performed through Almighty God's will." Then he tore his eyes away from her and raised his pallid hands: "And they entail the damnation of those that practice them!"

There were the childlike murmurs of "witch" again, but I heard other spirit noises and tried to follow them with my eyes in the church rafters, which creaked like the planking of an old ship. Gleams from the casket were blinding me.

Belle's not dead!

"It was not for nothing that the Salem trials of old '92 allowed spectral evidence, for spiritual sights are the proof of the spiritual life around us. God allows witchcraft sometimes to work. We do not claim that the tragedy in Salem was right. We can be mistaken, but we *must* believe the story in *Samuel.*"

My head whirled faster, and Lizzy shook me, alarmed. I was in a trance and steered my eyes about the nave. Lizzy banged and banged

my shoulder with her fist across Judy Rhines' large bosom to wake me
and stop my acting the lunatic in public before I was arrested for public drunkenness. Judy giggled and distracted the preacher from me. I
looked back at the world from my trance, and I knew all that went on
about me. Lizzy tried to get Henry's help to rouse me. I smelled the
wind roll off the North Atlantic. The voyage, the dead owl. The boards
creaked more. I tried to remember Belle's face, but couldn't, till I
looked at Moll.

Hammett dropped his voice to a whisper: "Friends we must
remember that the persecution of witches can be unjust. We must not,
like some here, go about swimming reputed witches just because we're
afraid."

I could hear laughter behind us, and Hammett's ironic tone was
our old vengeful God. Hammett closed his eyes and added ambiguous-
ly, "We *must* be just before God."

The timbers creaked: "Yes, Yes, Yes. Yes."

Henry too seemed to have heard the assent of the church. He
joined in nodding "yes" in rhythm with the timbers. Neil was silently
clapping his hands. Moll was looking at the roof beams, wide-eyed.
Some people jumped up, and feet echoed in the vault like cannon. Judy
unleashed a short guffaw and pretended to cough.

In my mind, I slowly exploded every joist and beam of the tower,
while protecting the congregation in the nave.

"It is believed that the Great Lisbon Earthquake of 1755 was a
punishment for the witch persecutions. But nevertheless we cannot . .
.." Hammett stopped. He looked right into my gaze, seeing everything.
He knew I had him.

Hammett craned up at the roof tree, as if he had forgotten what
he was going to say.

"The drink has got him," said Lizzy, biting her lip.

Belle gave me power. I prayed aloud, "Colprizana, Offina, Alta,
Nestera, Fuaro, Menuet!"

Crack!

The great kiss of death!

The congregation clattered up and stampeded for the doors, screaming and trampling each other to get out. Parents rolled over their children to protect them. Reverend Hammett was the first to reach the side door to the tower, but it was jammed, and he was forced back into the church, looking to see if anyone had noticed his aborted flight.

Shouts echoed through the crowd like the sudden burstings of fireworks.

At one end, the roof showed through, and the dust of old wood filled the church like brown smoke.

"Tower's fallen!"

"Tower's done collapsed!"

Many of us leaped out windows. This eased the crush at the doors. Finally, we were all outside.

Roger who had gone out to smoke his cigars had almost been killed by the falling tower. He threw his lit cigar at me.

Because of the catastrophe, we were hurried to the grave site. Most were too upset to attend the service in West Parish. But we watched Belle lowered into the earth.

Then we walked fearfully back to the Commons. There were more catcalls of "witch." A few rocks were tossed. Neil and I walked backwards to protect Lizzy and Judy Rhines. After we passed Thomazine's on the Fox Hill Road, we were safe.

I had destroyed our own church. Was Belle leading us to life or death?

"Tomorrow night," Judy Rhines whispered to me. "Sabat at Whale's Jaw. We have to protect ourselves now. We're in grave danger."

We parted. Judy and Neil took Lizzy home to Scot. I went to the Boo to read the Black Book.

CHAPTER 24

What if Lizzy were leaving again? As I walked up the Commons Road to look in the house window, a rock struck my elbow.

I ran to the Boo and snatched my fowling piece from behind the door—luckily still there.

But when I came out, I was surrounded.

About eight youths circled me, some of whom I had seen in Philemon's Tavern in the village—I recognized Red's stiff soaped hair— even though they had painted their faces and hair like fall leaves and wore Indian blankets, pinned about their necks. Another unseen came up behind me and pricked my back with a knife. I dropped the gun and sneered. Fucking hayseeds.

Rather than bring me to the Harbor Village, they dragged me to Granny Day's swamp. I did not see a kucking stool, which would have been useless anyway, as the swamp was shallow. The leader—it was fat Roger—did everything by signals of the arm or gestures of the head, not saying anything, nor did the cider I could smell on him loosen his tongue.

When he flung his forefinger at me, the two muscular boys who were holding my arms twisted them and bent me forward. The other lads lined up and in turn had a swat at my nose and jaw. I went numb fast and only vaguely tasted the blood running into my mouth. I heard more than felt the next few cracks, though I feared for my teeth, as they loosened.

Then the blows stopped.

The two athletes pressed my head under water for about a minute. But I always could hold my breathing for a good two minutes, an old witch trick. Though when I was let up, I coughed and sputtered more than I had to, to let the yokels think that I had choked and that their young powers were strong. So they chuckled together for a good while before dunking me again.

The second time was much longer.

They thought they were drowning me this time, I made such gagging noises. And I looked so awful with the blood and all and began to jump about so twitchily they thought I was having a heart seizure. But I knew this ruse wouldn't work long, so after the third, longer kucking, I kicked low and hard twice. Then I fled across the field behind the swamp.

"Get the witch!" Red screeched, finding his tongue and fearing to lose the prize. But the known dark gave me an advantage. Behind, I heard two thuds off oxen standing in the dark. Then a big shadow shot up in front of me. Jesus, Black Neil! In the dark his size was immense, and when he stood up he looked like a thunderstruck red pine. He must have heard the ruckus, for he was carrying the old discarded bars to the Commons. He looked like a black Samson carrying a Gate of Hebron to Gaza. He rushed past me, charging the pack.

"He's conjured the goddam Devil!"

Neil's great horse tushes flashed in the dark, as he hurled the iron bars, knocked away the legs from four of them and slowed the rest, who were tripping and casting off their blankets.

Then Start, and some other wild hounds he ran with, drove the gang from the pasture. As they ran down the Commons Road past the Boo, a short ax swung back and forth on a rope hung from a tree limb across the road.

Neil screamed, "Swipe 'em, Jude!"

Roger screamed, "Judas!"

Once they crossed the Commons Bars on the west side, Abaijah and other dogs could be heard chasing them and barking and, no doubt, tearing at the leather of their shoes and boots. I heard the boom of Judy Rhines' voice calling after them: "You need more water for kucking than we got up here!" She then looked at me in a nurse-like way.

"I'm fine. Just dripping a bit," I said, my whole head numbed. But I was enjoying the pride of pain.

She rubbed her salve on my battered face; then she broke off a sprig of red maple sapling and knelt outside the bars. She held the sapling up to the sky and shook rain drops into the dark air.

In moments it began to rain. The sound was luminous in the dark, like small words bursting off the dark leaves, as if ghosts had been forced to speak. Then, though it stopped as abruptly as it began, it was healing, hypnotic, and made me forget all life, all pain. Pain was not real anymore. She began to rub my penis.

But suddenly I was so shaking with rage that should have been obvious to Jude and Black Neil, had they seen me in the daylight. Or did they see me? I now had the silent power of the rocks—silly as it was to say. Unable to speak, I was thirsty to deliver the village. The moment was here, though I had no idea what to do. But I was sure I had some power. That I had passed a great examination. Like the God of the Old Testament, I would be both Killer and Preserver.

Judy Rhines looked softly into my sore eyes. "Tomorrow, Granther. Tomorrow."

CHAPTER 25

Our site was Whale's Jaw, and our fire would be right under it. A dark day dissolved into darker evening. The rain was blowing from the southeast, till at seven o`clock it stopped. I walked on air to the site. The pain in my face dissolved. Neil had made a rough ladder out of two saplings and some branches and rope, and I climbed quickly to the top of one jaw.

Traffic along the road. Two dressed like Indians. I dowsed my torch in a cleft in the rock.

"What's that, Roger?"

"Just a will-o'-the-wisp. Didn't you see it? You're not afraid? You don't believe in witches?"

"No."

"But you're a bit afraid all the same, wetleg?"

"How many will we have tonight?"

"Plenty. We're gonna to clear these witch-people outa here, if we gotta burn 'em out."

I made out Neil hoarding firewood from the scanty copse nearby and blanketing it with a tarpaulin. I whistled "phoebe" to get his attention, then came to him and pointed down the road. Neil waved me off with a laugh. He fingered Devil's horns; then made a fist. He made five tens. We would outnumber them easily. Where were all these witches coming from? Neil was painted like an Indian too and wore fringed breeches, a deerskin jacket with gold coins attached with gray hair, probably from Tam. He had his ancient fowling piece strapped to his shoulder.

In my renewed torchlight, the two massive rocks that formed Whale's Jaw gaped palely in the dark, like some leviathan waiting for a victim. Me? The whale had just breached the earth, was still half-covered. Its eye, if it had one, was still buried. Some blind power, not knowing evil, breaking out, as if just reborn, a great fish, planted by the redmen for fertilizing the ground, suddenly breaching back into the world, only to be frozen half in air, half in earth, neither dead nor aware—jaws agape, ravenous for breath.

An ox cart arrived.

Thomazine, coughing and barely able to walk, helped by Judy Rhines. They brought a large cauldron and blankets for the ground. The cart must have been filched.

Neil set up the firewood like a tiny teepee under the Jaw, took my torch, and, as the fire licked up, I could see that the faces of Thomazine and Judy were anointed with black grease. I climbed down and embraced them. Judy Rhines carried a great mask head of a mastiff. She said nothing but plunked it down over my head.

"Satan to the life," she said.

Judy spun me around, and I walked into several boulders before I found the peepholes in the mouth. By a flick of my eyes, I could bury myself in animal darkness and brood.

"It's Sammy's" said Tam, "The essence of magic's transformation."

"Yes," I said, "transformed." A tube slipped down my throat. Dire, bitter with acid, like Judy's rum, poured down my unswallowing throat. Yes, yes! Was I the pig in the sty?—no matter.

"Bring the hand," Tam said.

Neil brought a little bundle and unwrapped a partly rotted hand: The Hand of Glory! But whose? It had to be the hand of a criminal. Reading my thoughts, Neil said, "It doesn't bang his pistol on the desk, anymore!" The bank pirate—Epes Wilson! Neil put it on a low rock, palm down, saying "Looks like it's picking up money, don't it?"

"Wait till the bank boys see this," Judy said. "Don't forget to pickle it with horsehair, Neil."

> *The hair of a mare in heat*
> *Will double your golden treat.*

"You'll be rich for sure now, Neil," Judy Rhines said.

"Shut yer mug, Jude," Thomazine said. "Life's a joke *almost* to the very end."

"Rude Jude," she answered.

"Shut, slut" Thomazine snapped, and Judy Rhines could not speak.

Thomazine set up the severed hand on its back on a low rock before the fire. It had decayed to the color of tweed. She twisted fat into little wicks at the end of each finger. I began a chant from The Black Book, but failed to remember it. I girded my loins and recalled how Adam and Eve had to have made up their prayers long before the Bible came. Perhaps all prayer was made up by people and just revered by later generations. How would anyone know that my prayers were not authentic, if they were good? Then, in the firelight, I saw Belle in a white dress waving to me to come after her. Suddenly the right words came out of me.

> *Amen.*
>
> *I conjure thee, thou deadman's hand,*
> *By sky, by Hell, and by each planet,*
> *By sun and wave, by breeze and land,*
> *By gold, silver, all beryl and granite,*
> *Grant us the powers that we demand—*
> *Now, light this wood at my command.*

Not bad. Tam lit the fingers, and the Hand of Glory blazed down the tunnel of my dog muzzle, as if I had been a powwow making a fire with my voice at the end of a cave. Transformation *was* the essence.

It was Thomazine, drunk, who was reciting verses now, though they sounded more orthodox than mine:

> At the spell of the dead man's hand,
> Sleep all who sleep! Wake all who wake!—
> But be as the dead for the dead man's sake.

More gathered in the dark. In the fire, I made out some who had left the village long ago. Alison Millet, that half-insane girl whom Scot once reluctantly tended, came into the firelight with a wriggling Start, who must have turned up at her door, and her Aunt Smith, who made our dire, came under a head of unbonneted white curls. Ali was disguised as a princess, with a conical hat and attached veil. Aunt Smith was a tinker, hung with cups and pans. Judy passed me a bedsheet and a hay-fork wand. I attached the sheet at each end, climbed up the Jaw and let it ripple proudly in the wind, sailing for a new, undiscovered continent.

Others were gathering too. Phony Indians stalked about the trees and hid behind the great rocks. One looked like constable Call, and another was the blond Lanesville boy from Sam Gilbert's store.

I saw him creep in, and grab Neil's gun.

Neil saw too and waved me off with a shrug. What did he think I was going to do? Play target on Whale's Jaw. I tried to climb down. He waved me back. Was he trying to kill me? Neil slunk off and passed easily among the "Indians" in his costume. A moment later a great dwarf appeared in the firelight with the fowling piece. From his gyrations I recognized Sammy Maskey, his legs healed.

Standing on Whale's Jaw, I looked down at the ensemble and felt like John Eliot about to preach to the Indians. I imbibed their savagery, as he did when he preached the Bible to them in their own languages. I was to be teacher and preacher and general, but I felt my glass legs tremble on the slanting rock. I could easily take a fall down the sides of the jaw, a laughable Jonah tossed to a whale of rock, scraping a knee or bunging an ankle to the delight of Judy Rhines, my dog mask falling off and my being seized by the "Indians."

The rain in the leaves hissed at my cowardice. The wind growled, and the feral dogs and the great sea farther off blended all sounds. A mist baptized the rocky jaws and made them shine in the firelight. Now and then, a dead branch could be heard snapping.

Run, run away now before it's too late.

In fact, she's dead.

Black grace drove me on—the ritual was for others who did not know the secrets, who wanted to believe in spectacle, who couldn't lead, who wanted to perform. I swept my wand and sail through the air to stir the hearts of the mob. I still had an anxious hour to wait before ten o'clock, the time of the assembly when I would recite in torchlight. Everything felt sacred, even when I urinated down from Whale's Jaw and aired my privates to the wind. Others, seeing, cheered me on. The sacredness of our baseness! I thought with sympathy for Presbyterian Lizzy mortified. This was my life's graceless pinnacle, what Providence had kept me for. After, I would be tossed to the dogs and rocks, like Ahab. Yes, the rocks were alive, just waiting to move, dissolve, in their own good time, the way window glass sinks and bulges over the centuries. The rocks had surely moved since I had been there. We needed the rocks; we would miss them.

Beyond the circle lit by the fire, shadows danced. Now was the moment of madness, if I could live up to the part, and scare off the town or stir up the others against them. These needed a show, too. Recklessness pays off, doesn't it? Thomazine's madness kept her in fat. The reckless power of the powwow surged in our witch blood.

Neil handed round dire jars. He climbed Whale's Jaw and poured some more down the long tube inside my mask. The acid taste was in it again, and the heavy, wet air made the air smoky. Thomazine croaked: "Saint Elva sails." I threw off the deadening effects of the dire and the cold threats of the Indian shadows in the woods.

Moll Jacobs arrived hauling a white goat. The goat skipped about when it saw the fire, but Moll soon hobbled him. She wore a shooting outfit of bright green with leather leggings. In the glow of the fire, she again took on the glow of Belle reincarnate. Moll had even tinted her hair more reddish-gold and spread it like Belle's along her shoulders. She mounted the goat and rode about.

Even more now came in disguise. This made me falter, as they could have been more from the Harbor, but Thomazine hailed them by reassuring false names: Vaycheon, Stimulamation, Orasym, Aglon, Soter. No one recognized the bearhead that had a familiar laugh, till Henry revealed himself. Surely we would outnumber the kuckers from the Harbor Village. We must have been more than two hundred now. Soon we would outnumber the dogs too. But we were almost unarmed.

Start and Abaijah began howling at the trees and rocks where the "Indians" were flitting from tree to tree. I fumbled down from the rock with Neil's help and over Tam's protest. I snatched two burning firebrands, one in each hand. As I strode, I slashed the air in front of me, burning and x-ing my way through the crowd toward the woods where the town toughs were—relying on numbers to back me. Where did they arrive from? Were the Indian shadows afraid? Was I safe? No matter, I was a powwow fire-writing on the dark, sometimes blind as Samson because of the shifting headgear, and shouting the "Be gone!" of the exorcist. The town boys stayed still behind the trees. I could not tell how many they were. The pains in my knees subsided with the excitement.

The dogs now gathered behind me, led by Start. There they stayed, a barrier between us and the town boys.

I began to climb back up the ladder onto the rock as majestically as glass legs could unaided. We would have to wait it out. The occasion would have to teach me what was needed. I could not climb back up with grace, though, and felt the indignity of a crab crawling over a rock, a poor leader for the coming confrontation.

Neil stepped forward. His war paint shone in the fire. Then he turned and approached me backwards. "Great Elva," he cried to the assembly and me but most to the town: "Great Dog of Dogtown. Our town has lost First Parish"—cheers from Thomazine—"We have lost jobs, lost the road. They call us witches and want our land: we have lost our good names. We must avenge ourselves."

"So mod it be!" They pronounced the last word, "bay."

"So mod it be!" All cheered madly, till their voices shrilled to a long, deafening scream that crescendoed, then died away on the slow wind.

Sammy brought out wood models of a barkentine and a large house with a gambrel roof. He set them down in front of Neil.

"An incantation against Gloucester!" I shouted and looked for response from the shadows and the trees beyond the fire. Nothing. They were waiting.

Black Neil pulled two brands from the fire and propped them on the ground unevenly with rocks so that they resembled a upside-down slanted crucifix, like that on which Peter was nailed. He put on more billets till it flamed upwards. Then he placed on it the barkentine and the gambreled house.

"So mod it be," cheered the crowd, and their words echoed off the frozen shadows of the rocks.

"The powers of darkness grant your request," I said, assuming my pretend bishop's voice. Moll snapped several hairs out of the lurching goat and threw them on the fire, that sparked a tiny rainbow, and Judy Rhines, not to be outdone, threw on some live toads and mice that she had brought in a mason jar. The models and offerings were consumed and left only faint locks of smoke.

"The town will love us again," Sammy Maskey whined out at the dark to provoke them.

"Elva," Thomazine cried, "I have helped us greatly."

"Tell us, Apora," I said, blessing her with a new name.

"I have sent the auxiliary fire brigade to Salem." The shadows moved closer. Who were these growing shadows, witches or town boys? Our numbers had to protect me now.

I took the lead again, "On what ruse did you send them, Apora?"

"I spread the word that the British were burning the city. But I lied." All laughed heartily.

I said, "Excellent, Apora. It will ease our way."

"And fires will blaze unchecked," Sammy Maskey cried.

"The fire is there," screamed Judy Rhines, as she pointed back to the trees, where a will-o'-the wisp gleamed.

"It's a sign," I said.   The dire was working—and the ecstasy. Sammy tended the cauldron to distract himself. Some brought fire buckets full of water from nearby houses for the soup. I had doused water! Neil threw in: "Gunpowder and leeks and cabbages."

"The heads are boiling nicely," said Sammy, warming to the work.

Groggy, Thomazine suddenly awoke and groaned, "And where is the salt?"

The cry was taken up in all its sarcasm. "And where is the salt?" echoed off the rocks, and even the shadows and rocks yowled it.

"Dogtown can afford no sea salt!" Sammy Maskey cried.

"The food is so bitter without salt," laughed Neil.

"Terribly, terribly, terribly bitter," the witches answered, as they lined up with their bowls.

"How sour my brew," said Sammy Maskey laughing and walking up and down, as he sipped through the mouth hole of the dwarf mask.

I waved my wand and sail and cried, "We shall not starve. Dinner is served."

"Dinner is served" ripped through rocks and far shadows like the ninth wave and it was taken up even by the boys behind the trees. The witches sat on the ground and ate, as at common tables in an Old-Country village.

I awaited the attack.

But no rock was tossed. They were still being entertained. Sammy Maskey now held the gun ready. But nothing moved from behind the trees and great boulders.

Judy Rhines spat soup at Black Neil, who spat back, calling for the missing salt, and others followed. All chanted their laughter into one long howl and then, breaking abruptly, swilled sloppily and lustily, sharing even with the village "Indians," the dogs parting to let them through. Moll "gave birth" to a cabbage by taking it out from between her hunting leggings and holding it up to the fire, then throwing it in, while Sammy Maskey clapped and danced alone.

Neil stuck burning black candles to the rocks about Whale's Jaw. When the candles were dowsed by rain or wind, Sammy rushed breathlessly about to relight them with a burning brand.

With renewed legs, as on that night when she jumped into Granny Day's swamp, Thomazine climbed to the top of the ladder and handed me up a great marzipan cake on a molded board, along with Neil's ax. I tilted the cake to the congregation. It was shaped like a hound. All barked like dogs and madly the dogs echoed them, till I raised the ax like a monstrance above the congregation, and they kneeled in sheepish mockery.

"Our body and blood lies in this marzipan," I shouted.

I then cut the cake with the ax and passed squares down to Judy Rhines, who distributed them. "Through this cake," I went on, enjoying myself as I went, "our lips are sealed against all torture. We shall never say what happens tonight, even to our selves." This would help spread the news of the sabat. "May the Devil be blessed!"

"So mod it be!"

"May King Elva reign for ever," Sammy Maskey declared in a tone of solemn consecration. Then he danced off behind the trees and rocks giving some cake to the village boys who ate and laughed and ate.

So it echoed through the woods: "So mod it be!"

Deep down in the dogmask, I reveled in my powers. The mugs of dire went round and up and over and down. Then Sammy added, "We shall defend our king!" and "defend our king!" was the many-headed antiphon soughed in the trees and rocks deep back into the woods.

Moll Jacobs stepped forward, waving a fowling piece and throwing it to Henry, the bear, who chased her pretending to shoot. She began dancing with Neil, backs into the circle, counterclockwise; then white-headed Aunt Smith and Henry joined in the same fashion, as did many who no longer thought they could dance. Sammy Maskey went reveling through the linked arms, bowing and scraping, a jester dwarf herding wallflowers into the ring, including Alison Millet.

Rocks dissolved into mist and gray smoke and reformed again and then were disemboweled and spun off through the woods. The rocks were mists; mists rocks. Noticing the miracle, Sammy was weeping, as if personally mocked by the melting stone, as if the village itself were dissolving. I signaled to Moll to volley at the sky with her fowling piece. She swung the gun to heaven and blasted like a sudden drum stroke.

A pause like thought—then all resumed with greater vigor.

Moll drifted out of the dance circle and stripped herself of her shooting outfit. I threw her the sheet, and she wrapped her nakedness and, half hid in Whale's Jaw, began to dance till she looked like the Virgin swaying with her child, but she was holding Start, who had wandered back into the festivities and was miraculously calm in her arms. Moll eyed Henry, now drunk, and he went behind the rock with her. The dog ran back out. But Henry was too inebriated apparently, for Moll danced back out too soon after.

The dance still whirred on, on still. Judy too was naked now and joined Moll beneath the sheet. Moll and Judy danced like a twin-headed snake and caressed each other's shoulders, the sail staying wrapped about them like skin, as Sammy Maskey howled, like a dog, in heat. Start joined in Sammy's howl. My legs twitched wildly. Whale's Jaw was truly Hell Mouth.

I was aroused, my leg wet and icy. This was beyond my acting. My ear was ringing with the constant scream of unbroken laughter. Sammy clambered up and poured more dire down the mask. I sat on Whale's Jaw, dazed from the acid of the drink and the lack of air in the mask, from the flickering faces in the firelight, from the licking heat of the Hell Mouth of fire. I had stepped beyond.

Then the Indians attacked. I saw them down the long mask, rushing among the witches. A brave threw something at me.

"Come up, Granther. Peace is here."

I gaze up at Belle in a white gown on the tip of Whale's Jaw. I scramble up and take her proffered hand. She sits on a throne carved out of Whale's Jaw stone, and I sit beside her. She is on my right, and Lizzy, now drunk and laughing, is on my left and pointing at me, laughing, mocking. Belle smiles without opening her eyes. I stand quiet before her like a dutiful child, totally at peace. I smile below at Henry lying in the smoke with a succubus, whose dog-toed feet protrude. A whole field of folk opens up when the smoke steadies itself upwards, and I can see clearly, though it is dark. All eat rotten cabbages cut up in urine-smelling soup.

A scarlet glow reddens the whole field. Another dance begins. Another white goat brought by Moll Jacobs appears and stands on its hind legs and grows taller than Peter's Pulpit and has long horns that curve up and back and blazing eyes. It has Judy Rhines' face. The dancers, sky-clad, shower her with crushed bayberry leaves. Thomazine leads, youthful and sprightly. Soon she is rewarded with an incubus in her arms, a demon with the bottom half dog. The dancers whirl facing outward around Whale's Jaw, hands joined, backing into the fire circle. Common lovemaking now begins: I and Belle, Lizzy and Henry, all, all on the wet ground, lovemaking. I have lost mastery.

All quiet. Music lifts from the woods. "I'm gonna do what the spir-
it says do." Plaintive echo of viola and whistle of wind about the boulders
and drum snap of fire with barbarous dog-howls. Judy Rhines, the great
goat, waves at me to keep away from the dance. The dancing owns me,
leading, following. Through the Devil's dance I weave the pack, and they
wind their circle faster and faster, faster and faster. The fire spouts a river
of sparks up to sky. Night-piercing screams that no one hears nor feels in
the lightness of limb and in the banging of the heart. Unstoppable return
to the forest. The shadows come forward and dance. One by one they fall.

The goat with Judy's head churns out of the dance, charges Belle,
falls, veil rent, and with a horn punctures her heart. I try to grasp her,
but the dancers bump and kick me and my arms are locked by
Thomazine on one side and by Henry on the other. Finally free I reach
Belle to raise her battered body up. But she rises by herself, singing for
the dancers, but her words are muffled by the whine of a dog off in the
dark. Stunned, she wobbles about with a hazel wand blessing the assem-
bly, the goat following her as torch-bearer. Henry is pointing me on. I
can't go forward nor back. The smoke diffuses. Soon there is a wall of
smoke everywhere.

I wake in the dark hollow of the dogmask. Shame overwhelms me:
I have become the most destructive of gods: there is no more village or
society or morality or…

I lay on the wet ground below the goat's great weight. I had fallen
off Whale's Jaw and lay on the ground. My hand ached where a rock
struck it. I pulled off my dog mask that softened my fall: I was cheek
to jowl with my son, Scot, lying on top of me, crying, shouting, "Don't
father, don't." I threw him off and climbed back up Whale's Jaw. I
regained my seat.

"Our dances have ended!" I shouted to the few drunken, exhausted
and emaciated revelers, most of whom were asleep. Many were already
gone. The rest obeyed like cattle. There was no sign of the "Indians."

Smoke, cold and hardening, melded with dawn and whitened into the boulders, leaving open dark spaces between. Scot sat up and looked about. Then he pointed to a bundle. At the foot of Whale's Jaw was the corpse of Abaijah. He had been shot by the village boys.

The Dies Irae was bonging on a church bell, like a call to arms to pass Last Judgment on me for my black deeds.

CHAPTER 26

In the distance, church bells kept banging the alarm. A cold pink light smeared over the rocks. As Scot and I entered the Commons Road, Henry called to me something from the dark wood I could not hear. Still the bells clanged, clanged the Dies Irae.

Henry called out, "For the love of God, the Harbor Village is on fire!"

Scot looked at me horrified. How could there be a fire in this wetness? And the militia was away in Salem! We ran back to the Commons Settlement. Everyone was up in the village. Without questioning me on the events of the night, Lizzy got me some scraps of food and some clothes, saying "Go, Granther. Go, help!"

The sky was full of pink smoke to the south, and firelight lit the bottoms of the low clouds. Henry kept crying: "Good God! Good God!

Granther!" His words stabbed my heart; had I become so forgetful of conscience, as I had of pain? And if Henry might turn against me to gain a foothold in the village? Again remorse bit into me. Hadn't I killed a man, trying to be a hero and had I now burned a city out of pique? I would be swum well this time. I had to hang on—no matter what the "Indians" would do to me in the Harbor Village. Neil and Judy Rhines had brought the two oxen and cart they stole for the sabat and waited in the road near the Boo. Sammy Maskey brought four fire buckets from outside someone's door.

"What are they for?" Judy Rhines laughed "For the fuel?"

"For mockery," said Sammy Maskey, back in his bonnet, "Just gleeful mockery."

I said nothing. But revenge had fled my soul. Need. That was my food now. To be needed, to be useful, to help, to save—that was what had been there all the time growing beneath the rocks.

Jude dumped out any water and turned over the buckets for seats. So we rode in haste to the Harbor Village: me, Neil, Jude, and Henry, Sammy staying to calm Scot, who wanted to go, and Lizzy. I rode in front with Neil. Start crisscrossed under us like a dalmation.

At a bend in the path, Scot jumped in, no doubt sent by Lizzy. I saw he had on his Spanish-leather boots. He sat glumly in the back, taking stock, saying nothing, looking puny.

Judy said, "It is our triumphant re-entry into the city—our Palm Sunday—and Start's our herald, Herald of Dogtown! Lord! Lord!"

The glow on the southern horizon looked like a jack-o'-lantern filling the sky, burning up the low clouds, like auroras. The rocks on the south side were now dimly reflecting the fire, like burning lava chunks from a volcano blast.

Speechless now we turned into the Fox Hill Road. There we met the blond Riverdale boy on Gilbert's wagon, no doubt on high hire, coming from the Harbor and carting an exhausted family of six, their furniture tied on. He wore a long, straw hat pulled low to cover up his remaining Indian paint.

"What's happened?" Neil asked.

The boy was anxiously alert. "Witches—I mean Indians—have burned the town," he shouted and urged the team on toward Riverdale. But the oxen couldn't move.

"Leave me alone," he hissed beneath the turned-down straw brim.

"Forked tongue," Judy Rhines snapped. Then released her spell.

We rolled on towards the conflagration.

"Sun comin' early this morning," Judy sang, improvising a song.

Henry, getting jumpier as we neared the Harbor, countered: "Hurry, Neil. People need me there." The church bells still throbbed their condemnation. Would they need *me*? Would it be my just punishment? I began to relish the thought of punishment and purgation.

"Men out mackerel fishin' too," Neil said.

"The militia at Salem!" Judy Rhines guffawed.

The exodus from the town jammed the road. People were fleeing towards the heights of Cape Ann, where, from the headland, they could safely view the fire. A river of horses and wagons and wayfarers and screaming children streamed around the ox cart on either side, like a panic-stricken flight of gypsies. Our struggling, opposing lines of force were unforgettable.

Despite the dampness, many women lay with their children in the grass beside their household goods to ease the shock of the fire and the wayfaring. Some camps were already set up.

When we reached the town, we saw the fire devouring Front Street. The burnt trail led back to Gilbert's outfitting shop.

"The oilskins spontaneously combusted," Neil said. "Happens."

My legs relaxed, and I breathed easier.

In the street we saw a fire pump with a raised tub of water with a hose spout on the top and pump bars in front and behind. "Miracle!" Judy Rhines exclaimed. It was like a great witch's cauldron, as if ours had flown there by transvection and had grown immense. Henry raised his hand to slap her but looked about and thought better of it. A few men and many women and children carried fire buckets from the basin to the westerly lip of the fire, its living end. Gilbert's store had long been eaten away, and the arms of the fire, like a willow of flame, now fell on Lowe's Tavern.

"Good riddance. Let it burn out. It's only a dry husk now," Henry shouted, trying to win favor with the teetotalers. But no one would listen. He suddenly stopped shouting, hung his hands at his side, looking like a sick cormorant, and waited for someone to tell him what to do. I let the fool hang there without consolation. His magic was dead.

Judy Rhines gloated: "A bonfire of their hotels and fancy roofs with widows walks! Burn their ships! Rotten sailor bastards! God bless fire!"

A line of stores along the beach was already reduced to old wasp nests, while the conflagration had leapt the road and ran its course toward Middle Street. The whole Harbor Village lay open and defenseless. Henry looked at me pleadingly. More women were evacuating their homes, loading their wares on wagons that had come from the countryside and were charging three-dollars a mile freight. It was Gloucester's Hell.

"Tam'll become rich, if they go by Dogtown," Judy bellowed.

Fires now burst out like shells spontaneously from the backs of buildings, so we could no longer see where the fire line was. Horses charged into the flames, and we could hear their screams as they were burned to death. The remaining horses had to be led out of the town. I blinkered the oxen. Nonetheless the noise spooked them, and they might have run wild, if Judy did not soothe them with devil names. Neil wanted to let them out for hire, but consented to put them in the custody of the constables. The firelight and the shadow made me think of myself still in my dogmask, and I waved the ox goad, as a wand. A picture flashed into my tired mind. I thought of the exodus from the Harbor that had passed us, the counter stream flowing against us coming to town. Butt back!

Then I saw the "Indians" arriving with some buckets and with some paint left on. They looked at me with hatred. There were about twenty of them. They were uncertain what to do in front of the town and looked nervously at Neil.

I took them by surprise.

"Two lines," I shouted, "two lines." My voice caught a lull in the din, for everyone turned and looked. For a moment I really thought I had on my dogmask, but it lay somewhere back at Whale's Jaw.

Being at a loss, the onlookers obeyed, even some of the Indians. People mechanically lined up. I had found the right word. "Two parallel lines," I called out, "men here, women there."

And two parallel lines there were.

Judy Rhines mocked on: "A contredanse, Neil, a contredanse!"

I glanced at her now with hatred. Neil too looked at her savagely. Judy merely laughed and danced with Start, whom she held by the forelegs in the crowded street, happy to let the town burn down. But my days as Vengeful God were gone.

As if aware of my powers, Judy stopped her joking and, letting Start go, she joined the ladies' empty bucket line.

Some of the boys stopped, including Roger, began to pelt us with rocks. But Scot, who lived among the rocks his whole life, fired back with painful accuracy, striking and splitting Roger's lip. Then they stopped.

I went on as one hypnotized, gestures and orders breaking from me spontaneously in orders to the firefighters. The fear of the fire eating the town overcame me—I wanted to save, even to sacrifice myself if need be—and even the kucking boys fell into lines, as I ordered. Like the flow of fugitives from the city, I pressed all into two contrary flows. The Principle of Return! Butt back. I shouted, "Faster, men haul the water; women send back the buckets. More buckets! More! More!" Water was hauled all the way from the ocean.

I now climbed up and took charge of the pump basin from a scared Indian that I recognized as Red.

"Keep the cauldron—tub—full."

Whether it was God or the Devil that gave my legs strength, I stood on the tower, as on Whale's Jaw once more. I held the delivery pipe between my legs and sent spurts of water curving down against the fire. Under Neil's direction, two boys on front and two on back worked the pump bars. Even one old man who looked much older than the country itself hauled a bucket, slow but sure. It was Reverend Hammett.

We moved the wheeled tank after the living fire. By now Hammett's vicarage lay in the flame's path, beyond some chestnut trees. In panic, Hammett climbed up beside me on the fire tower, weeping and pleading to direct the hose nozzle, but it wriggled serpentine in his hands, drunkenly lashing the empty night air with water. Henry tried to help him, but, in my new authority, I pushed him away. As Hammett and I touched hands again, our eyes met and Hammett blanched. I saw the same look of pale guilt I saw on Lizzy's face: the deadly fear when she thought of Thomazine. So Hammett believed in witches and was afraid in his dirty Christian soul that he was no match for witchcraft. Murder will out. In his face was Belle and Moll and who knows what else. I had my vision, and my heart rebounded in power. He saw punishment at hand.

He wavered.

I held my sword of fear and water over Hammett's head. Hammett's eyes pleaded for home and life. The power to bind and loose lay in my hands. For a moment I went all comical. I wanted to laugh to beat the Devil, like Jude. But purpose quickly chilled me. I looked straight and unwavering into his shifting eyes. Then Hammett made the Devil's bargain, and let me have the hose to myself. He saw the raw fearlessness in my eye, and I saw the terror in his soul—the foolish bastard! He remembered what happened at Belle's funeral. As he backed down, he kept Henry back too.

I called, "Midael and Mirael."

And Roger called back "Witch," but everyone was too occupied now as the fire rose hotter at first from the water of the hose. As the hose spouted stronger from the increased pumping, I rode a waterspout that leapt into the dark sky. Then the smoke back-drafted, and a smoke explosion made a wall between us and the fire. I could see nothing. My eyes burned, and my throat clotted. Where was the living tongue of the fire? Hammett's vicarage would be charcoal in minutes if the fire attacked directly. Through the smoke screen, I couldn't tell distance. Bats shot out before the flames.

A shingle of fire flew up in a clearing in the sky; below it was the pink smoke from the flaming vicarage. Its reflection from the burning building helped me judge the direction and distance of the fire. But it was no flying shingle. It was my owl Hoppo returning and reflecting the fire below her, leading me to the fire's tip! Then I began to sicken from the smoke, but Scot jumped up and helped me cleave the river of smoke with the stream of water in the distance, still judging by the brightness of the fire on Hoppo's breast, as she circled and circled above us, watching for escaping rodents. A barrier of chestnut trees broke into flame, and we could see clearly that the fire had blanketed another row of houses, Reverend Hammett's being one.

With Scot helping, I slowed the fire and soaked Hammett's vicarage. Soon the tip of the fire roared its course another way. As the wind veered, I saw the flying white shingle of Hoppo swooping for mice and shrews driven into the street.

Other sudden outbursts of random fires continued, till one was the rising sun itself.

I was a filthy aureole still on the tower, when engines arrived from Ipswich and the brigade returned from Salem with their equipment to extinguish the low burning by noon.

By then, I was no longer a witch. She had perished in the fire. And all my hatreds had perished too. They were poor rabble also now, just like us in Dogtown Commons, many reduced to poverty by the fire. The Harbor had suffered enough: 60 stores and 40 homes lay smoldering. There would be now much to do in the Harbor Village with the rebuilding. We would be as useful and as welcome there as angels. I saw Roger and Red, sitting exhausted in the street—just poor, defeated, ignorant boys, in need like all of us. We needed each other, witch and priest, town and village.

It did not take long for Reverend Hammett, still deathly afraid of me and my spells, to come to my rescue and invite me to be of service in the rebuilding of the town. I saw how his words quelled the gathered Harbor boys, who were getting ready to rock us again for the fire.

Reverend Hammett would buy Dogtown now at any cost. They needed our houses, our wood, our help. He looked like Death Conquered in the biblical engravings. An apology shivered through his long skeletal body. I felt that we could all move to Gloucester now; fear would always be something to give me the punch of power. Witchcraft would sleep again, until it was needed. So this was where Belle delivered me.

. . .

On the way back, I, Scot, Henry, and Jude slept in the cart, Start's head on Jude's lap, even the banging of the wagon did not wake them. Neil drove. The ride was slow, and I too dozed.

When I awoke, I found Scot holding the reins and Neil sitting in back asleep. Henry was mumbling to him, "I must begin again. Too much reminds me of Belle. New work must be done in the Harbor. We must learn more about witchcraft, and we shall learn more of Reverend Murray's Universalist ideas there. And I can study the dogs, too."

I climbed in front beside Scot and saw Scot's Spanish-leather boots ruined by scorching. He must have been helping in some burning building. He seemed not to care.

Neil woke. His eyes looked wild and ran with red rheum. "There is money there still. I know there is. I'm staying. The land's good. Land's good."

"What, Neil?" asked Henry absently.

"In the buried ground, under the boulders of the Commons Settlement. Captain Kidd's gold. The buried gold."

CHAPTER *27*

When we returned, it was late afternoon, and the ocean blew cold wind. Spring had held back. The village appeared shabbier than ever, now that I was to leave it. Every season always looked like fall here. Old leaves skittered about, red and gold autumn remnants that stuck in the deep rifts in the boulders and in the potato pits of the vanished houses and in the exposed cellar holes with their scattered foundation stones, always the same ashy leaves, as if the great hand that had scattered the boulders there had thrown an old pumpkin and it had shattered over the Settlement.

The gray rocks looked like immovable chunks of ice, but the river of rock would always move unseen. I felt more than ever the crawl of the stone, the gigantic lurch of tree and rock at the bottom of an invisible current. I felt one with the rocks now, as if they were old ancestors

that I no longer had to worship. The great rocks might once have had
the faces of respectability, but now had cracked and veined, some split
by trees, growing right through them, as if they were ships, masted and
scuttled. I had landed for good.

All was expansion, movement out, in mind and body. The sea
smell was in the air and told me *move*, like the cold wind, as sea and
wind once did leaving Portsmouth Harbor for a poorer world. The yellow bulbs of early May barely pressed out of the boughs above the dead
leafage.

I looked at Scot, and he smiled his understanding.

When we arrived home, Lizzy was tying clothes in bedding.

"Where are you going?" I asked.

"The hell outa here!"

Then I felt as if rocks had been rolled off me. I hadn't realized my
ease earlier with Scot. I mastered more than witchery but couldn't use
the word with her. I looked at Lizzy and saw one more lamb caught in
between the rocks on Lamb's Ledge. She was as sad as Belle and more
earth-bound. I could help her and Scot now. For a minute, I could not
speak. Then I realized that we would have to help each other, all in all.
Without my witch powers, I was just a weak creature, too.

I said, "We're going to the Harbor. Scot will work there, after all."

My voice was so matter-of-fact and cheerful, Lizzy looked at me
thunderstruck, smiled doubtfully, and said nothing. Then she lowered
her long nose and cried, cried to wake the dead, as she did when she
forgave me for being sent down from Harvard, as she wept when our
children died. When she finished weeping, she looked years younger.

A week later, while I was taking tools out of the Boo, I met a cart-
load of furniture and firkins of dire. Beneath was Aunt Rachel Smith,
our dire maker, and Alison Millet, her half-daft niece, both of whom I
had seen at the sabat. And Scot.

Aunt Smith said, very business-like, "Scot says they need us all
now. They're building up in the city."

"And they need your dire," I added.

So "up in the city" was now the Harbor Village. So be it. Alison winked at me, her eyes full of bright light. She seemed less mad now that she was leaving the spell of the village. She said, "Scot said he would help us unload and set up tents outside the Harbor."

I said, "That's a great load, neighbors. Good to have some extra to pay the toll."

"Toll?" Aunt Smith said.

"Thomazine's."

"Why, Thomazine's down," Aunt Smith said.

I was silent a moment.

"Nonetheless," I said, "I can see a wheel come off your cart when you pass her house." They laughed and rolled off.

. . .

We ourselves left the following week, Lizzy looking girlish in her new thinness, as her spirits had returned with the Harbor prospects and a sense of a future. She rested her head upon my shoulder as I drove, since I no longer, as Judy would say, "stunk witch," since she had burned in the fire. I gave our house to Moll, Judy, and Neil because theirs was no longer livable and they did not want to live with Thomazine. There were limits to my powers, as Thomazine had said. They wouldn't leave because they hated the Harbor so terribly. Sammy Maskey would look after them.

We lived in a tent camp, and rebuilt houses with the money collected in Boston and elsewhere. Start soon ran off from the Harbor back to the swelling packs he was used to, so I often visited Dogtown looking for him. Sometimes I saw him or heard his yelp on Lamb's Ledge and worried he might be wedged among the rocks like the lambs. The next winter I often found Moll, Neil, and Judy Rhines sleeping, covered with a blanket of snow, for Sammy never caulked the cracking walls properly.

Judy would ever be sneering at Moll, and one day in my presence, she said to Moll, "I shan't tell you where I hid the cards. I hid them in the chest, but I won't tell you."

But Moll growled, "We don't need fortune-telling anymore. Granther has delivered us." Then she turned to me and said, "Belle wanted it this way. She approves."

One day Sammy had gone out to do washing and did not return, making off with the bedding. Scot brought them more from the contributions to Gloucester. Constable Call wanted to take them all to the almshouse. But Neil refused to go and threatened to throw Constable Call off Whale's Jaw.

When I returned later that winter, dogs were everywhere, no longer differing in breeds, for many had hybridized into a mass of moving coffee-colored pelts that blended with the landscape. Pieces of that landscape broke off and leapt at my hands while I walked about, recalling my old training and expecting food, for they went without both, since game was now depleted. Soon it would be too dangerous to travel without a gun. Neil was gashed on the cheek again, as he slept in the snow in the half-boarded-over old Lurvey cellar.

Neil stayed that winter. He was not at the house, when I went to visit him one zero-degree morning. I found him again asleep and frozen in the Lurvey cellar, his ax still beside him where he went to look for money, his frozen face grizzled like snow on dark granite.

Lying on top of him to warm him, I woke him.

He mumbled, "Where have the doubloons gone, Granther? Where are those bits of eight hiding?" He fainted. I was so angry I could have killed him with his own ax. But instead, my long pent-up tears burst like tears of blood.

When I finished my "womanish" weeping, I remembered the black henbane that was still in my pocket. Like the year before, I rubbed it on Neil's wounded face and frozen feet, but it would not work, so I got Constable Call and had Neil taken to the poorhouse. His toes were frozen and could not be saved. He died within a week after the amputations.

Thomazine died on the fourth day of February. She had contracted pneumonia, and the hard cold of that year took her. No doubt Jude's removal tormented her. She was seventy-six years old, but it seemed she had always been old and stories went around that she was at least fifty years older than that, but had preserved herself by eating a mixture of beet root, kelp, honey, and herbs, for which she would never reveal the recipe. Judy Rhines claimed it was dire that preserved her. In fact, when she died, many refused to believe that she was really gone, and it was said that she was soon seen again collecting her tolls on Fox Hill.

As a makeshift cabinetmaker, I was called upon by the Overseers of the Poor to do the coffin. Scot helped me, so he could start a trade. The snow had turned to sleety rain and turned the road from ice to half mud. I still wouldn't sell my Boo, so we worked there and sawed, spokeshaved, and nailed the pine into a coffin. Carefully we rubbed in burnt umber stain with a rag and then polished it over with beeswax to perfection. The sleet crashed against the door like an angry sea clambering over the headland.

I helped Lizzy to lay out the body, she still being afraid of Thomazine, even in death. I stared at Thomazine's nakedness, cleansed for the first time in years by vinegar. Did that dried leaf of skin over frail bones have secret powers? Was this what the Harbor feared?

And still did.

Judy Rhines wanted all the best for the coffin and the funeral, so I borrowed from the now-obliging bank on my future Harbor prospects. The coffin was furnished with a pure silver nameplate and silver clasps, like Belle's, and there were to be liquors and Bordeaux on hand at the funeral, not just the usual rum.

I assembled Judy, Moll, and Henry with my family and a few other mourners, and we buried Thomazine, alias Apora, beside Abram Wharf on Wharf Road, buried her with honor and Christian prayer. I chiseled a cross on a huge rock beside her.

On top of the rock, Hoppo landed for a moment and flashed her white wings.

Then, she headed back north for good.

THE END

BIBLIOGRAPHY

Anon. <Susan Babson>, *Along the Old Roads of Cape Ann* (Gloucester, MA: McKenzie, 1923).

John J. Babson, *History of the Town of Gloucester, Cape Ann* (1860; rpt. Gloucester, MA: Peter Smith, 1972).

Roger Babson, *Cape Ann Tourist's Guide* (Gloucester, MA: McKenzie, 1945).

Francis Blessington, "Afloat in Dogtown Moraine" (poem), *Wolf Howl* (University of Missouri—Kansas City, 2000).

———————————————— "Dogtown" (poem), *Lantskip* (Dublin, NH: William L. Bauhan, 1987).

———————————————— "Paper Like Snow" (poem), *Connecticut River Review*, 13 (1992), 15.

Alfred Mansfield Brooks, *Gloucester Recollected*, ed. Joseph E. Garland (Gloucester, MA: Peter Smith, 1974).

Melvin T. Copeland and Elliott C. Rogers, *The Saga of Cape Ann* (Freeport, ME: Bond Wheelright, 1960).

S. Foster Damon, "Witch of Dogtown: A Drama in Three Acts" (Unpublished play at The John Hay Library of Brown University, 1955). (Performed in Gloucester, 2-4 September 1954.)

Thomas Dresser, *Dogtown: A Village Lost in Time* (Franconia, NH: Thorn Books, 1995).

Joseph E. Garland, *The Gloucester Guide* (Rockport, MA: Protean Press, 1990).

Marsden Hartley, *Soliloquy in Dogtown* (exhibition catalogue) (Gloucester, MA: Cape Ann Historical Society, 1985).

Britta Karlberg. *Dogtown, Cape Ann, Massachusetts: A Guide to Sources* (priv. pr., 2000).

Herbert A. Kenny, *Cape Ann: Cape America* (Gloucester, MA: The Curious Traveller, 1998).

Percy MacKaye, *Dogtown Common* (New York: Macmillan, 1921).

Charles E. Mann, *In the Heart of Cape Ann or The Story of Dogtown* (1896; rpt. Gloucester, MA: Ten Pound Island Book Company, 1990). The 1906 reprint contains the useful appendix, "Beginnings of Dogtown: Data From Days Before the Village Was Deserted."

Charles Olson, *The Maximus Poems*, ed. George E. Buttrick (Berkeley: University of California Press, 1983).

Eleanor Pope, *The Wilds of Cape Ann* (Boston, MA: Nimrod, 1981).

James R. Pringle, *History of the Town and City of Gloucester* (Gloucester, MA: priv. pr., 1892).

Irving Sucholeiki, *A Return to Dogtown: A Look at The Artifacts Left Behind by Some of Cape Ann's Early Settlers* (priv. pr., c. 1992).

ACKNOWLEDGMENTS

The following have either kindly answered relevant questions or graciously read the manuscript and made valuable suggestions: Sharron Cohen, Leslie and Matthew Cooney, Kitt Cox, Wayne Franklin, Joseph E. Garland, Herbert A. Kenny, Wendy Lindsay, David C. McAveeney, P. Carey Reid, Guy Rotella, Ted Tarr, and Ann Taylor. Thanks also to the staffs of The Cape Ann Historical Association, The Department of Archives of the City of Gloucester, The John Hay Library at Brown University, and The Sawyer Free Library of Gloucester.